ALARICK
One Night Will Never Be Enough

BY
JULIA MILLS

JOIN THE CLAN!

Wanna keep up with all my crazy? Have fun? Win some cool prizes? Get *exclusive* excerpts to upcoming books?
Sign up for my newsletter <u>RIGHT HERE</u>!
Be the FIRST to see new covers, sneak peeks, and best of all, ADVANCED COPIES OF ALL MY BOOKS!!!
Join the group! <u>Julia's Mills' Fan Club on Facebook</u>!
I absolutely LOVE stalkers! Here's all the links! Follow me everywhere!
<u>Newsletter</u>
<u>Website</u>
<u>Facebook</u>
<u>Instagram</u>
<u>Twitter</u>
<u>Pinterest</u>
<u>BookBub</u>
<u>Goodreads</u>

ACKNOWLEDGMENTS

Edited by Em Edits
Proofread by Book Nook Nuts
Beta Read by Linda Levy

To my girls, Liz and Em, I Love You. Every day, every way, always.

ALARICK

Sharp...Successful...Deadly...
Catering to every dark, erotic desire of his wealthy patrons
has made Alaric a very rich man. His ability to tap into the
very soul of each person, to see what they yearn to possess...
intimately...sensually... has made *CRAVE* the most sought-
after establishment of its kind in the world.
A force to be reckoned with and Scottish to the bone, he
carries the tattoo of a fire-breathing dragon wrapped around
the left side of his body. This shield, along with his bond to
the Universe's chosen warriors, the **Dragon Guard,** serves as
a constant reminder of what was taken from him.
Driven to excel...to *always* remain in control...
he's *never* been defeated.
But the Past is a cruel mistress who demands her due, no
matter the cost.
Fate refuses to be denied... Some demons simply refuse to
be slain...
And Life, no matter how long, rarely plays out as planned...
Running from a past he can't escape, lost to the insanity of
the **Thirst** - the scent of home, of buttercups and poppies,

invades his senses, momentarily clears his mind, and demands that he find the one woman...the *only woman*, who can deliver him from certain death...his **Bloodmate.**
This is a Vampire's Thirst... Dark...Dangerous...Undeniable...
One taste will never be enough...

1

*S*talking *through the abandoned structure, warm blood dripping from his chin and staining the front of his stark white shirt, he reveled in the game of cat-and-mouse the pathetic humans continued to play. The scent of their fear, the pounding of their hearts, the whoosh of their warm, succulent life essence as it flowed through their delicate veins was intoxicating. The thrill of the hunt was upon him, and nothing would keep him from claiming his prize.*

Standing in the hallway, inhaling deeply, the long-forgotten growl of the predator he'd locked away so long ago rumbled within his chest. Long, sharp, and deadly, his fangs once again slid from his gums. Scratching and clawing to be set free, the beast rose to the surface, refusing to be ignored.

They were close. The heavenly aphrodisiac of their terror hung in the air teasing his scents, arousing his desire. Pictures of them hiding, holding one another in the darkness, praying for their very lives flashed in the chaos of thirst and need that was his mind.

Throwing back his head, his arms spread wide, fists clenched so tightly his nails tore through the skin of his palms, the ancient vampire let his rage fill the empty halls as he roared to a God who'd long ago abandoned him. Tonight, he would finally be free. Tonight, the beast would feast.

Slamming the heel of his boot through the large wooden doors to his right, lured by their scent through what was left of the splintered wood hanging from the rusting and creaking hinges, he ripped through the room, a predator hunting his prey.

Tossing the rotting, forgotten furniture aside as if it were no more than children's toys, his ravenous gaze landed upon the young, nubile women, foolishly thinking they could hide from him. Huddled in the corner, their bodies curled so tightly he couldn't see where one ended and the other began, the women's screams reverberated off the barren walls.

Lunging forward, he fisted their long, tangled tresses, and yanked their heads back until they could go no farther. His cock hardened as his canines ravaged the first woman's neck. Hot, sweet, and coppery, the blood flowed across his tongue, igniting his every sense like the finest port.

Draining the first dry in moments, he let her useless corpse fall to the ground as his focus shifted to his second victim now unconscious in his grasp. Shoving her head to the side, he drank his fill, his erection painfully hard as it pushed against the zipper of his pants.

Blood...Sex...Need...Rage...

Over and over he drained his victims, one right after another, seeking release where there was none. Hunger, thirst, desire, bled together, a fantastical morbid mosaic that became a living, breathing entity within him, refusing to be quenched.

Following the thunderous beat of the last remaining heartbeat, he reached into the darkness. Stifling her screams with his hand around her neck, already tasting every drop of her blissful blood as he snuffed out her life, his fangs tore at the tender skin of her neck...

"Alaric!" The voice slammed into his consciousness.

"She's mine," he snarled, the talons at the ends of his fingers connecting with skin and bone, the blood of yet another victim flowing down his arm.

Jumping to his feet, letting the woman's lifeless body crumble to the floor, he scanned left and then right, searching for the bastard who dared to interrupt his feeding. Scenting the stale, fetid air, he sifted through the stench of decay and rotted flesh, smoke filling his lungs as the voice returned, roaring, "Wake the fuck up! You're going to burn the place down."

Reaching from the depths of his nightmares, Alaric's fingers tightened around the thick, corded muscles of a man's neck, fantasy and reality battled for control of his mind. Nameless, face-less bodies littered the ground at his feet, his eyes landing on the last body, the most important, the one he'd been searching for...

"No!" He bellowed.

Bursting forth, throwing off the hauntingly vivid visions that dogged his every step both day and night, his eyes popped open, immediately meeting the steely stare of his longtime friend and Second-in-Command, Ruari, as the younger vampire snarled through gritted teeth, "Kindly remove your claws from my neck."

"Claws?" The word had barely crossed Alaric's lips as his eyes snapped to Ruari's neck.

Retracting his deadly talons, Alaric's mouth watered as he watched the fresh, crimson trails of blood flow into one at the base of his friend's neck before disappearing under the collar of his black *CRAVE SECURITY* T-shirt.

"Like what you see?" Ruari growled, getting to his feet before adding, "What the hell is wrong with you?" Pointing to the silver, stainless steel trash can at the far side of the bed, he went on, "You haven't lost control of your fire in centuries. Are the Dragons close?"

"No," Alaric grunted, climbing out of bed, refusing to look at the other man. "They are not." He strode across the room naked, his dick hard and his shoulders thrown back, refusing to make excuses or acknowledge the demons that were chasing him. "And I will thank you to but the hell out."

Walking into the bathroom, trying to slam the door on yet another reminder of how far he'd fallen, Alaric stamped down his contempt as Ruari's beefy palm on the wood stopped the slam he so longed to hear. "Talk. Now. You're a fuckin' mess."

Glaring at his friend, thoughts of ripping out Ruari's throat and leaving him on the floor to bleed out, Alaric refused to speak. Pounding heartbeats, the succulent scent of fresh blood filled his senses as the club's employees began to arrive. Snapping his jaws shut to hide his extending fangs he gave the door a final thrust, leaning against the cool wood and letting out the breath he'd been holding.

"This isn't over," Ruari spat a split-second before the ringing of the bell of Alaric's private elevator echoed through his penthouse apartment letting him know the younger vampire had thankfully stormed out.

"Aye, no truer words were ever spoken, my friend," he mumbled, wiping the sweat from his brow. "God save my worthless soul if this shit gets any worse."

2

"I really, *really* don't want to go to this party," she blew out the breath she'd been holding while putting on her mascara. "Isn't it enough that I'm wearing a bright yellow, organza monstrosity Cecily called a bridesmaid's dress? Why do I have to go to her bachelorette party, too?"

"Because you've known her since you guys were in third grade. It's the right thing to do and... You're a nice person." Ash's best friend Leslie winked at her in the mirror from over her shoulder. "And let us not forget, you need a night out. Time to face the world with that dazzling smile. What's it been...three or four years since you did anything more than dinner and a movie with me or Cecily?"

"Oh, shut up," she grumped, fixing her bangs then turning her head side-to-side to be sure her blush was even while trying to convince herself that she was going to have fun.

It wasn't that she didn't want to go out, maybe even meet a nice guy, fall madly in love, have a few little ankle-biters and live happily-ever-after. That had actually been her dream since she was old enough to clomp around in her mom's high heels and paint her lips with pink lipstick. However, being the youngest pediatric cardiothoracic surgeon in the southwest, a woman and having a cute baby-face was not conducive to finding a mate.

The last guy she'd gone out with had spent the first fifteen minutes of their date reading her profile from google. "Dr. Ashlynn Annalissa Aimsleigh, Triple A to her friends and family, is a renowned cardiac surgeon not only in the United States but also abroad. In her undergraduate years, she graduated Summa Cum Laude from Harvard with the third highest GPA in the university's history. Going on to complete her graduate, doctorate and medical training at the prestigious Johns Hopkins University, she then returned to her home state of Texas after and is presently the youngest ever Head Surgeon at Children's Medical Center Dallas. She has been..."

That was where she tuned out, sipped on her margarita and acted like she couldn't hear him over the music when he asked how much she earned a year. Why was it that men always asked two things after they found out who she was – her gross yearly income and if she'd ever 'done it' in an operating room?

"Stop thinking so hard, Ash. Take Dr. Leslie's orders and have some fun." The tall, thin blond she'd known for most of her life handed Ashlynn a cold bottle of Corona, the lime already floating on the clear, amber liquid. "I am ordering you to have at least one drink every thirty minutes until the break of dawn."

Snickering despite her misgivings about setting foot in the club *D Magazine* called, *'The most decadently hedonistic experience in the state of Texas. You don't have to wear leather to feel the heat. Whether you're a voyeur or enjoy hands-on plea-*

sure, CRAVE is the place to be' Ash had to admit she was curious to see what lurked behind the dark windows and sleek lines of the club that seemed to appear out of thin air and always had eager patrons lining up around the block.

Then there was the club's owner, the single-named, drop-dead gorgeous, mysterious millionaire known as, Alaric. Of course, the editors of Dallas' trendiest magazine had not only featured him on the cover but also had a complete six-page spread inside. Sales for that issue had to be the best the publication had ever seen. Hell, Ashlynn went to four newsstands just to get her copy. The moment she'd seen his face, she'd been compelled to possess a copy.

It was as if his photo had jumped off the page, demanding to be adored. Alaric had immediately become Ashlynn's guilty pleasure. She'd hidden the magazine in the stack of medical journals beside her bed, just in case any of her friends made an impromptu visit, then stared at it nearly every night. It was the first time she'd drooled over a guy on a magazine cover since she'd been in middle school and purchased *Teen Beat*, but she just couldn't help herself.

The weight of his stare, his eyes the perfect blend of cobalt and ashen charcoal, made her heart skip a beat and her temperature rise. Her fingers ached with the need to explore the wide set of his shoulders and muscular biceps that tempestuously tested the strength of his starched, light-blue, cotton shirt of which he'd roguishly turned up at the cuffs.

Jumping from her thoughts as Leslie cleared her throat, a sure sign she was losing her patience, Ashlynn countered, "How about one an hour and I limit myself to beer? Will that satisfy Dr. Party Pants?"

Nearly spitting out her Corona as she barked with laughter Leslie teased, "Damn straight, I'm Dr. Party Pants. I have a Ph.D. in Boogie-Oogie-Oogie and a specialty in Hot Bods."

"Oh my God." It was Ashley's turn to burst out laughing. "How old are *you*? Boogie-Oogie-Oogie? I can't wait to tell Cecily and the others. Maybe we need to stop at the Thrift Store and get you a pair of platforms and a neon-striped tank top."

Throwing her hand in the air, Leslie chuckled, "You're just jealous. The girls will be dazzled by my wit and brilliance. You know it's true."

"You know I do. I live in awe of you." Clicking off the light, Ashlynn followed her best friend down the hall. "Do you have your purse?"

"No, not taking one and neither are you." Grabbing the bag from Ash's hand, Leslie tasked, "Good Lordy, Girl. You can't go to a club with an overnight bag." Lifting the large mocha-colored leather purse up-and-down a few times like it was a weight, she added, "We gotta travel light. There will be butts to squeeze and chests to explore. Have to keep our hands free." Dropping the purse, she waggled her eyebrows. "Put your debit card and cash in your bra, your phone in your back pocket and lipstick in the front with your keys." Grabbing Ashlynn's hand, she whooped, "It's off to the Den of Debauchery we go."

Struggling to keep up while stowing her belongings where her bestie had instructed, Ashlynn groaned, "Are you sure these pants aren't too tight? I can barely get my phone in my pocket and don't get me started on this blouse. I swear my boobs are gonna pop out the top. A wardrobe malfunction is imminent."

"Hush and come on. You look like a rock star," Leslie pulled her out the door. "Your body is bangin'."

Looking over her shoulder, Ash scoffed, "Bangin'? Have you been hanging out with your 'crew' again?"

"Oh, shut up. I can't help it that I teach Sophomore English to a bunch of inner-city thugs." She laughed. "You know I love those kids." She shrugged. "Besides, they teach me the coolest things." Chuckling, she added, "Now, stop deflecting. We all keep telling you that you have an awesome figure. Men love curves. I have no clue why you hide it under baggy scrubs and a lab coat."

Locking the door and shoving her keys into her pocket, Ashlynn snickered, "Ummm, because I'm a doctor."

"Yeah, okay. Just promise me you'll chill out and have some fun. Seriously, Ash, you need it."

Making up her mind to take her friend's advice, Ashlynn gave a single nod and emphatically agreed, "Yes, I do." Slipping her arm through Leslie's, she added, "Let's do this," as they hurried towards the taxi waiting at the end of her walkway. "Tonight, I am just plain Ash. No Dr. Aimsleigh in sight. Watch out world, here I come."

3

Opening his second bottle of his special blood/Merlot mix, Alaric filled his chalice and turned towards the floor-to-ceiling windows behind him. Tight and overheated, his skin so sensitive to touch that he stood naked, gazing at the twinkling lights of the spectacular skyline. Hell, he couldn't even touch the soul of others anymore. When he tried, all he saw were the horrific visions of him draining them dry or fucking them senseless or both.

Add lost my fucking mind to the list of ailments and rip the heart from my chest. This bastard is down for the count...

Images of a huge, stone and mortar castle, the stronghold of Iain MacLauren, the Chieftain of *Monadh Criobhe,* filled his mind. The enticing scents of sea air, fresh rain and heather filled his senses. The caw of the gulls and the sound of horses' hooves thundering across the countryside echoed within his mind, precious memories from a time long forgotten by most. So far away, both in time and space, but so very important. Every second, every action, every step had led him to this place, this time, this uncontrollable, all-encompassing need threatening the entire world he'd built from the ground up.

The pitter pat of little leather soles on the cold stone floors of one of the bastle homes where his father's soldiers slept awaiting the next battle resonated through the long, narrow halls. "Whaur ur ye, Bastien? Aur ye hidin'?" The high voice of his six-year-old self called out mere seconds before he squealed with excitement.

"Aye, Ah'm hidin' froom ye. Is 'at nae th' point oof thes silly game?" His father's Second teased, his baritone rumble tickling the young boy even more as the mountain of a man picked him up and swung him around.

"Tis', but noo tis mah turn tae hide."

"An' soo ye will wee lad."

But he never got to as the blast of the battle horn ripped through the air and Bastien, along with Alaric's father and the other warriors, donned their shields and swords and rode off into battle. Running as fast as he could, a young Alaric followed the men of Monadh Criobhe until he could no longer see the tails of their thoroughbreds through the early morning mist blanketing the moors.

Sitting on a stump at the far end of the MacLauren Clan lands until the sun disappeared behind the rolling hills and the air turn bitterly cold, he trudged back to the main house, shuffling in through the kitchen door and dropping onto the stone hearth in front of the fire. "Whaur hue ye bin, Alaric, mah booy? Ah was wooried sick."

"Ah were..."

The rest of his words were lost in the swirling as many lifetimes of memories raced towards yet another recollection. Stopping so abruptly, his hand slapped upon the thick glass as visions of a battle he'd hoped to never again witness glared at him like a specter from the deepest, darkest recesses of Hell itself.

Blocking his enemies' repeated attempts to take his life with his short blade, Alaric struck down all comers, his broadsword perilously gripped in his other hand. Stepping over dead bodies, casualties on both sides, he battled the heathens who five years earlier had taken his father from those who needed him most.

Fighting to protect the land belonging to their Clans and Tribes from the warmongering Romans, Alaric and his men engaged with not only other Celtic but also Germanic tribes from Cimbri and Teutones to protect their strongholds on the Jutland Peninsula. Trying to fill his father's shoes, he fought for his people, but also to avenge the death of the greatest leader the Celts had ever had by slaying Onitus, the Roman General whose blade had ended Iain MacLauren's life.

Looking over the shoulder of the man whose head he'd just removed, Alaric saw the pompous Leader of the Roman troops, sitting atop his stallion, smiling at the carnage, smirking at the men lost in the name of their Ruler, Gaius Marius. A red hue fell over Alaric's vision. Stone-cold rage filled his body. Racing towards the General, jumping over the lifeless corpses of the men he'd grown up alongside, learned from, thought of as kin, he focused only on the man responsible for his tremendous loss.

Closer and closer he sped, his eyes connecting with Onitus'. Vengeance, the fiery, undeniable sister of Revenge raced through his veins. His father's voice echoed in his mind, "Whit's for ye'll no go by ye. Fight fur bluid. Fight fur reit. Fight til death."

Raising his broadsword, slashing with deadly accuracy, his blow sadly missed its mark as pain shot from high under his right arm, setting fire to every nerve ending as it raced through his body. Falling to his knees, an enemy's blade lodged in his side, nearly piercing his heart. Alaric watched helplessly as Onitus rode forward, extended his right foot and with a swift kick to Alaric's head, laughed, "Today you die and the MacLauren Clan with you. You are Hell's fodder now."

Gasping, blood bubbling up his throat and filling his mouth before flowing freely over his lips and down his chin, Alaric struggled to move, to get to his feet, to avenge his father's death, to somehow save the day, but it was not to be. On this occasion, Onitus had been the victor. Alaric would die on the battlefield along with his men, his father's memory and all Iain had done for their people evaporating into the ether.

Long, treacherous hours later, the death rattle slowly vibrating deep within his chest the only sound he could hear in the dark, desolate corpse-filled meadow, Alaric gasped as the sounds of horse hooves invaded the last moments of his life on Earth. The footsteps that followed made his dying heart pause for several seconds before finally giving another sluggish beat.

Kneeling down, a dark-haired, fair-skinned man wearing the plaid of Clan MacAngoran from the Highlands, kin who had been wiped out by Gaius Marius' army years before, asked, "Whit hae they done tae ye, Brither?

Unable to speak, trying with all his might to move away from the demon the devil had sent to taunt him in his last minutes, Alaric gurgled and spat, fresh blood rolling across his dry, chapped cheeks as he tried to roar at the ghost.

"Dinnae fear. Ah hae bin sent by yer seanmháthair. Th' mammy of yer maw felt yer need an' wants yoo ta' live anew."

The *ding* of the elevator jerked the ancient vampire from his memories as he downed what was left in the silver chalice and turned to stare at Ruari.

"Has the dress code become more, um…" he motioned up and down Alaric's body with his index finger, "lax? Have you got the permits for complete nudity, Boss?"

"What do you need?" Alaric cut to the point, stepping forward and pouring more wine.

"You have a VIP waiting in your office." Ruari's voice was laced with tension and more than a bit of anger, something the ex-Commander kept well-hidden even in the worst of times.

"A guest?" Alaric handed his friend the bottle of wine and shoved a clean goblet across the highly polished, mirrored bar top. "You know I never make appointments during operating hours and most definitely *never* in the club."

"Yes, and so does this person." Ruari took a sip of Merlot, looking over the rim of his glass. "But then again, Clarence never was one to follow directions unless they were those of the Directive, and his newest protégée, Mateo, is no exception." Continuing to stare, he inquired, "Something you want to tell me?"

"What the fuck is *he* doing here?" Alaric asked, ignoring his friend's question, instead making a show of once again filling his goblet before returning to the window. Shoving the torment feeding on the anxiety that the name of the Directive's new investigator added to his already chaotic emotions down as far as he could, Alaric summoned every ounce of his waning control.

Wasn't it enough that he did everything possible to stay off the radar of the *one* organization in all the world that controlled Supers, the ancient Vampires that have lived among the humans for centuries, can pass for an ordinary person, and are well established both in business and society? Once would think, however, it was never the case. The Directive always had to poke and prod and try to dig up dirt on any and all Supers that they could. They loved playing judge, jury, and executioner. It was an aphrodisiac to them.

Living among the shadows, never revealing the location of their headquarters, enlisting the brightest, the best and the oldest among all Vampires to police everything supernatural, they were nothing if not diligent. The Directive was the worst kind of Internal Affairs and most assuredly the deadliest. But then again, he couldn't argue with the need for some kind of policing authority, he just hated being the one who they were investigating.

There had been a time when a Coven or Clan could go out and kill a village or two before the sun came up with no repercussions for their actions. If Vampires wanted to be regarded as anything other than monsters, there had to be rules, and the Directive took pride in enforcing said guidelines.

"I have no idea. You know they regard me as your lapdog. The prick walked past Security, tapped me on the shoulder and with the same shit-eatin' smirk he was sportin' when we had the formal introduction a few months ago, said, 'Tell your boss I'm here,' then headed towards your office."

The sound of the bottom of Ruari's glass striking the bar's wooden top was just a little too forceful. Alaric knew it was to get his attention, but he wasn't into games, especially not with his hunger and sexual need rising exponentially with every beat of his heart. Leaving the view of his beautiful city behind, the ancient Vampire headed towards his bedroom, calling over his shoulder, "Tell Mateo I'll be there in five. Let the bastard wait."

"Aye, aye, Boss. Any other errands you need me to run? Your dry cleaning? Groceries? Want a mochacinno- kiss my ass -frappabeano?"

Usually, Alaric found their brotherly banter entertaining, but on this night, visions of reaching through the hardwood of the door and tearing out his longtime confidant's heart flashed in his mind.

"Ya' know we still have things to talk about," Ruari grumbled. "Starting with your piss poor attitude and flaming trashcan bullshit from this morning. I'm not letting this shit go."

Waiting until he could hear the young vampire get into the elevator and the door slide shut, Alaric whispered into the darkness, "Maybe Mateo's here to take my head. The Directive wants to make a statement. Shows their power and his prowess by letting his first kill be an Ancient. Let the dickhead make his mark with an oldie but goodie." Chuffing sarcastically as he crossed the room, opened his closet and pulled out a pair of jeans along with his favorite leather jacket, the ancient vampire added, "At least I'd finally have peace."

4

———

"How did Cecily pull off a private room and back of the house entry at the swankiest club in the DFW Metroplex?" Ashlynn whispered to Leslie as they, along with four other friends including the bride-to-be, filed through the back door of *CRAVE*. "I thought the people in line were gonna mob us when that huge bouncer got us out of the back of the line and marched up to the front."

"Don't you worry, we've got bodyguards," Leslie chuckled, pointing to the two musclebound men waiting for them just inside the side entrance to the club.

Looking at two of the biggest men she'd ever seen in her life, Ashlynn thought they looked more like they were going to eat them instead of protect them. Trying to smile at the mountain of a man with tattoos covering his bald head, arms, and back of his hands, not to mention thick silver rings braided into the goatee that hung down to the middle of his massive chest, she ended up quickly looking away when he winked. Seven-foot giants who looked like they belonged to Hell's Angels were not her idea of Security, and most definitely did not wink.

Stepping through the door, her eyes landed on the bald man's cohort, and the idea of making a run for the taxi stand sounded like a true winner. Resembling a Viking with long blond waves that touched the tops of his shoulders, a jawline that would cut glass, bulging muscles, and wicked blue eyes, he was definitely handsome but had an air of danger that freaked Ashlynn out.

"Are you sure they're not our captors," she whispered, trying a joke to ease her tension.

"Very sure, Hun." Leslie laid her hand over Ash's on her shoulder. "Cecily's fiancée may be a rich, privileged momma's boy but he's got friends in high places. These men come from none other than..." The slow, sensual beat of the music just on the other side of the wall reached a crescendo that drowned out what Leslie said next as they continued farther into the dimly lit club.

Figuring that Rodney, Cecily's soon-to-be husband, wouldn't let anything happen to his bride, Ash shrugged as the bald giant led them through a door and into what the glowing sign above the doorframe called 'Silk Fantasies.' It took a second for her eyes to adjust to the soft amber lighting, but when they did, she feared they would pop from her head.

Everywhere she looked there were couples doing what she could only imagine was dancing, their bodies intertwined in intensely intimate positions as they swayed to the slow, pulsing beat of *'Cry Little Sister'* from *The Lost Boys* Soundtrack. She'd never thought of the song as erotic, but as her eyes stayed glued to the dancefloor her cheeks grew hot, and her hips moved in a lazy figure eight of their own volition.

Jumping as Leslie's hand landed on her shoulder, Ash spun around, barely containing her squeal of surprise, as the other woman put her mouth next to Ash's ear and said, "Come on. I don't want you to wander off and get lost. Our room is down that hall."

Pointing across the room into a corner hidden in shadows, Ash followed where Leslie led, glad to see the rest of their party waiting beside the two hulking men. Nodding to the others in the party and mouthing, "I'm sorry," she stayed in step with the group as the music changed from slow and sensual to upbeat, popular tunes the farther they moved into the depths of the club.

Smiling as she immediately recognized *Blondie's Sunday Girl*, Ash sang along wondering if Dr. Crane, one of her colleagues who liked music on in the operating room, would never guess that one of his favorite bands was being played at a place like *CRAVE*. "Not on your life," she snickered under her breath. "He's too preppy-New England-old-family-money for that."

Thinking about telling him just to watch him squirm while he wondered how she'd gotten into the club, Ash nearly tripped over her own feet as their group came upon ten muscled hunks, lined up in a perfect row down one side of the narrow corridor. Their skin oiled to a high shine, each wearing some kind of leather straps across their shoulders and chests that made her think of gladiator-type gear, she made the mistake of looking down one man's body.

Not only was his soft, black leather loincloth barely more than the size of a handkerchief, but the black G-string underneath barely contained his semi-erect penis. Popping her eyes to his face, blushing so intensely she knew she was glowing, Ash's mouth went dry when the gorgeous man raised an eyebrow and suggested in a low, provocative tone,

"Why don't you meet me after the show? You're the sweetest thing I've seen in ages. I'd lick you all over."

Opening her mouth, unsure what to say, Ashlynn had never been so glad to see the giant with long blond hair. Ducking behind him, she hurried to catch up with her group as he warned, "This is a private party. Keep your eyes off the ladies and do your job, or I'll have to have a word with Alaric."

Happy to be away from all the action, Ashlynn's heartbeat had just returned to normal when they entered what their bald escort called, 'The Velvet Room.' Not sure what to expect but ready for the first of what she was sure would be many drinks, she looked at the floor to ceiling crushed red velvet covering the walls and the black leather furniture and for the first time in her life decided – what the hell?

"How ya' doin', Kiddo?" Leslie came up beside her, shoving a Corona into her hand and grinning from ear-to-ear. "Can you believe this place?"

"Not even a little bit," Ash sighed before taking a huge drink of her beer. "I'm guessing from what I saw and heard that 'Silk Fantasies' is the tamest room in the club?"

"Yes, that's absolutely right," the Viking grinned, sidling up to them and standing on Ash's other side. "I'm Sampson, by the way." Turning, he held out his free hand and added, "If anything that happens tonight makes you uncomfortable, all you have to do is give me the nod, and I'll get you out of here, okay?"

Shaking his hand, Ash smiled, "I'm Ashlynn, but you can call me Ash, and this is Leslie. The blond with the tiara is Cecily, the bride-to-be and the woman next to her is her older sister, Audrey. I'm sure you can see the family resemblance."

"Sure can."

"The red-head is Karen, she's a sorority sister of Cec's and the one with short, dark hair is Melissa." Ash leaned a bit closer. "The only one of us who's married with kids, but still one of the old gang from high school." She knew she was babbling on, giving way too much information, but that was what happened when she was nervous, and boy-oh-boy, was she ever nervous.

Looking back to Sampson, she asked, "What's your friend's name? Is he a vampire, too?" The words were out of her mouth before she could stop them. Gasping at her incredible faux pas, she stuttered, "O-oh m-my God. I-I'm so s-sorry. I-I'm such a-a..."

Laying his hand on her upper arm Sampson smiled sincerely as he reassured, "Please don't worry about it. To be honest, it makes it easier when people just ask instead of pussy-footin' around and trying to act like we're not who we are." He continued to gently squeeze her arm. "But I have to ask, how did you know? Usually takes people longer, especially with all that's goin' on in here." He snickered. "Or they never say anything and just whisper behind our backs, which, we can hear anyway." He tapped the lobe of his ear. "Super senses are part of the gig."

Worrying her bottom lip with her teeth, Ashlynn contemplated whether she should tell Sampson how she'd known or not. She and Leslie had agreed there would be absolutely no shop talk at the party. Ashlynn was supposed to be just a part of the gang, out having a good time, not worried about how many times a minute someone breathed or the color of the veins in their neck.

Dropping his hand and bumping her with his elbow, Sampson teased, "You're not a secret agent for an undercover organization here to take out all vampires, are ya'?"

Laughing out loud, feeling herself relax, Ashlyn chuckled, "No, nothing that glamorous I'm afraid." Deciding to fess up, she went on "I'm a cardiac surgeon. It's my job to notice things other people either don't see or don't recognize for what they are."

Narrowing his eyes and leaning his head down, the vampire asked in a hushed tone, "What did you see that gave me up?"

Pointing to the table in the corner, Ash suggested, "Why don't we go over there where we can at least hear ourselves think?"

Looking at his friend and tapping his watch, Sampson quickly nodded, "Yeah, that'll work. Axel says we have about twenty minutes until the first round of entertainment gets here."

Rolling her eyes when his back was turned, Ashlynn couldn't help but worry about the 'type' of entertainment that was on the way. Deciding not to worry about things she couldn't control and enjoy talking to someone who was actually interested in what she did for a living and not the balance in her bank account, the young woman got up on a high back, leather stool and set her empty bottle on the table.

"You want another beer before you give me a class in spotting vamps?" Sampson chuckled.

"No, I'm good. Not really much of a drinker. Never was."

"That's better for you. I never did understand how people could get completely smashed night after night. Seems like such a waste of time."

"Yeah, it sure does, and it never seems to lead to anything good."

"You are so right, Doc," Sampson readily agreed, going on to say, "So, spill. What gave me away?"

"The longer I spend time with you, the more things I see

that make you different from a healthy, non-vampire, your age."

"My age?" He snickered. "Do you have any idea how old I am?"

Shaking her head at yet another mistake she'd made talking to her new friend, Ash quickly corrected, "How about I say, the age you appear to be?"

"Perfect." The huge Viking grinned, motioning with his hand for her to go on.

"Well, at first I could see that you only breathe about five or six times per minute and the average human male's rate is approximately twenty times in sixty seconds."

"Wow, I had no clue."

"Yeah, and then there's the way your jugular stays almost flat against your neck. In most men with a physique like yours, the larger veins protrude, and I can see their pulse. That's not what I see when I look at you."

"This is fascinating, Doc. Tell me more."

Ashlynn was shocked at Sampson's attentiveness and the way he leaned in to hear, hanging on her every word. It made her feel good like she wasn't an odd duck for loving her job. Sure, there were no sparks or attraction between them, but just like her mom used to say – A person never can have too many friends. "There's the way you move. It's totally fluid, no jerking or muscle tension. You have a grace that contradicts your size. And...well, you're really fast." She tapped the short, square tip of the nail of her index finger on the top of the table. "Like when that guy made a pass at me, you were nowhere around and then *boom*, there you were."

"That is fascinating. I really want to talk to you more, that is, if you don't mind."

"I don't mind at all, but it looks like your partner is trying to get your attention." She pointed to the man

Sampson had said was named Axel as the Viking nodded with a chuckle, "Sure is. We have to go escort the first act into the room. The festivities are about to begin."

Trying not to show her sudden anxiety, Ashlynn grinned as Sampson winked and assured her. "Remember, all you have to do is give me or Axel a nod, and we'll be right there. No reason you should be uncomfortable just to celebrate with your friends."

"Thank you so much," Ashlynn accepted a big hug from the Viking then watched as he walked away.

Never one to be left out, Leslie magically appeared with another Corona and a mischievous smirk. "What was that all about? Hitting on the help?"

"No, I was not." Ash shook her head. "Sampson wanted to talk about health and wellness."

"And he just happened to know you were a doctor?" Leslie raised her eyebrows as she sat down, putting her margarita on the rocks on the table in front of her.

Thankfully, even though she had her doubts about what was about to occur, Ashlynn didn't have to answer as the room was filled with a blast of honky-tonk music followed by loud whooping and hollering. Turning her chair, the young doctor's mouth dropped open as she stared in awe at the six chap-wearing, bare-assed cowboys with Sheriff stars on their hats, silk floggers in their hands and fur-lined handcuffs hanging from their belts as they pranced into the room.

Leaning back after Leslie tapped her on the back and leaned forward, Ashlynn nearly fell out of her chair from laughing so hard as her friend confessed, "I'm ropin' and ridin' one of them stallions tonight, Girlfriend."

5

———

Slipping his arm into the sleeve of his jacket, Alaric finished the last drop of Merlot, poured and drank two fingers of Scotch then marched through his home into the elevator jamming the first-floor button with his index finger. The blood wasn't helping. The alcohol tasted like shit and did nothing to curb his appetite. Looking at himself in the mirrored panels, he saw the faraway look in his eyes, the sneer of his lips, and the tight clench of his fists.

"What the hell is wrong with me? If I weren't nearly two-and-a-half millennia old, I'd swear I was going through the vampire version of puberty." Closing his eyes, he ran his fingers through his hair, down his face, and across the stubble on his chin. "I've done nothing but devour bag after bag of blood, bottle after bottle of wine and jackoff so many times my hand is tired." Opening his eyes, he stared at the beast clawing to be free as the deep gray-blue of his eyes bled to red and the tips of his fangs peeked from under his top lip.

Images of his fantasies returned, the same he'd had in the shower. *Instead of his fist wrapped around his hard cock, he saw her massaging him from top to bottom, her lips swollen from his kisses, whispered puffs of her breath coaxing drops of precum to the surface.*

Testing his resolve, her deep brown eyes captured his as the tip of her tongue lapped at his essence. Moaning deep in her throat in unison with his groan of impatience, the beautiful creature on her knees before him slid his cock into her mouth as far as she could, the vibrations of her hums of delight nearly driving him to an explosive end.

Fisting the silken curls of her light brown hair, careful not to hurt her, but needing to stay standing, Alaric's head fell back, the muscles in his thighs trembled as his fangs erupted from his gums, the need to own her body and soul replacing his all-encompassing hunger for the first time in over a month.

Jerking his hand out of his pants, Alaric slammed his hand against the emergency stop button and leaned against the back wall, shaking off the visions of a dream he didn't understand but longed to recreate in real life. Letting his eyes once again slide shut, he took several long deep breaths, counting to ten on every exhale. There was no way he could meet with Mateo in his current condition. He had a hard-on he couldn't hide and looked like he'd been on a week-long bender. The man was not only trained by Clarence, but had been a warrior, an executioner, a doctor, a detective, a Tracker, and a Hunter for centuries before being selected to be trained as another appointed to 'dole out' the Directive's justice, a dreaded Enforcer.

Thinking of the first time he'd meditated, the only thing he hadn't tried to calm his hunger and his soul, Alaric recalled his grandmother by his side and Androu, his Maker, in attendance as Alaric, a newly turned vampire unsuccessfully fought the torturous bouts of bloodlust and the uncontrollable urge to fuck anything in a skirt. No matter how much reassurance his *seanmháthair* gave him, he simply could not reconcile his unquenchable desire to exsanguinate anyone with a pulse with emptying his seed into their bodies over and over with the teachings of his gods.

"It is reprehensible, seanmháthair. Ye havta kill me. Send me tae Hell," he cried, ripping the hair from his head. *"Ah am naethin' moor than a demon. Wa did ye nae liet me die oan 'at battlefield?"*

"Coz Ah loove ye an' Ah hae a friend comin' tae help ye."

Looking up at Androu, Alaric wailed, "Nae, nae heem. He's awreddy doomed me ta' torment. Ah need nae moor fruom th' likes ay heem."

"And no more ye shall have," assured the tall, broad-shouldered man who walked in from the far side of the room. *Stopping in front of Alaric he continued, "I am here to show you another way, to bind myself and that of my Dragon to you, to give you the peace you need to carry out your Destiny."*

The stranger's accent, clipped and precise like that of a Roman, intrigued instead of enraged Alaric, but not nearly as much as his words. "Ah hae a Destiny?"

"Indeed, you do. One that cannot be ignored." The stranger knelt down and looked Alaric in the eye. "I am Carrick, Leader of the Red Dragons. Your grandmother has been a friend to the Dragons for many years. It is an honor to repay her in any way that I can."

Kneeling, the man called Carrick who claimed to be a Dragon laid his hand upon Alaric's arm. The scent of smoke and ash filled his mind. Dragons of all colors, shapes and sized flew through his mind. He watched in awe as the majestic beasts defended their homes and their kin with stealth and fire.

His vision narrowing to a single red Dragon soaring over a blood-soaked battlefield, Alaric watched as the beast slowly descended, changing from the Crimson Dragon to the man known as Carrick before his feet touched the ground. Rage and sadness colored the man's face. Warring emotions filled his mind and body as he tried to understand the senseless loss of life.

Mile after mile, the warrior walked, praying to the Heavens for the safe passage of each man's soul. Weary, both emotionally and physically, Carrick stopped beside a small river for the night. Making his camp, he was alerted to the arrival of two strangers by the sound of their whispers floating on the evening breeze.

"Who goes there?" He demanded, pulling his broadsword from its scabbard.

Appearing out of the mist, a tall, lean man with kind eyes and a long beard stopped beside an older woman with hair the color of silver. Raising their hands in surrender, it was the woman who answered Carrick's demand. "Fear nae. We wish ye nae harm."

Her magic was pure and that of the Druids. Her accent with its lilting beauty carried the ring of truth that made Carrick lower his blade and offer them food and companionship. Days turned into weeks and then months as the three traveled the countryside looking for survivors of the terrible Roman invasions.

Finally, the Dragon was called home, but before he left, Carrick promised, "To you, Brygid, and you, Androu, I pledge my fealty, my loyalty, and my friendship until the day my soul is called to the Heavens. It matters not that you are Vampire and I am Dragon, should you call, I will come and those of my blood as well."

Slicing across his hand with a silver blade at the same time that Brygid and Androu did, Carrick held his hand over the fire watching the crimson drops of his life essence drop into the flames. "From this moment forward, may the Dragons be at your call. Your confidences shall be our confidences, and we shall fight alongside you as true brothers in arms."

Mirroring Carrick's actions, Brygid and Androu responded in unison, "Froom th' moment forward, we an' aw whoo come efter us shaa remain loyal tae th' dragons. We shaa keep their confidences as they keep oors an' fight alongside them as true brothers in arms."

Brygid then continued, "By th' magic ay mah people we ur bond."

Taking his hand from Alaric's arms, Carrick encouraged, "Open your eyes, Alaric, son of Agora whose mother is Brygid. On this night, you shall receive the Blessing of Ancients and the calm that comes from Dragon kin that is as old as time."

Opening his eyes, Alaric was shocked to see not only Carrick but the face of the same red Dragon from his vision hovering over the man's face like a brightly colored shadow. Unable to speak, Alaric nodded, unable to breathe as he felt the warm embrace of not only the man but his beast as sparks of magic, similar but most definitely unique in its power than the Druid mysticism of his grandmother, filled his body and soul.

"Blessed peace of the calm waters, blessed peace of the soft breeze, blessed peace of the quiet Earth, deep peace of a shining star, may it all be yours. Moon and sun, Heavens and Goddess, Earth and Fire, Water and Air pouring their healing light and love to you."

Nodding, Carrick coached, "Say it with me, Alaric. Feel the words. Believe their meaning. Absorb what is rightfully yours and calm the warring spirit within you."

Opening his eyes while still repeating the mantra he'd learned over two thousand years earlier, Alaric reached forward, touched the red Emergency button allowing the elevator to continue its journey downward. Watching as the door opened, a minute wave a calm just barely holding his thirst at bay, the ancient vampire strode out into the candlelit halls that led to his office.

Taking a deep breath as he approached the solid black,

six-inch thick oak door, Alaric slowly let it out as he whispered to himself, "Showtime and as Ruari would say, 'Never let 'em see you sweat'."

Opening the door, he stepped into his office exuding his usual calm, suave demeanor, the act he'd perfected centuries ago. "What an unexpected pleasure, Mateo. What brings the Directive's favorite Enforcer-in-Training to my humble establishment?"

"There never has nor ever will be anything that you are involved in considered 'humble'."

Bristling at the Directive's new kid's condescending tone, Alaric stopped at the corner of his desk and held out his hand. "I take that as a compliment coming from someone as well traveled as yourself."

Smiling as he shook Alaric's hand, Mateo's eyes showed no emotion. He was not on a social call; the Directive never was. Feeling the sting of the Enforcer probing his mind, Alaric let go of Mateo's hand and went to the marble-topped bar in the corner.

Lifting the bottle of Scotch, he asked, "Would you care for a drink before we get down to business?"

"No, thank you." Mateo's search of Alaric's thoughts halted as he added, "What makes you think I'm here on business?"

Snickering and shaking his head as he poured half a rocks glass of twenty-five-year Scotch, Alaric chuckled, "Aye, you guys at the Directive are all work and no play, so, just cut to the chase and save us both some time."

Pulling his phone from the inside pocket of his perfectly-tailored black suit, the Enforcer slid his finger back and forth across the screen several times before raising the silver device and showing Alaric a picture of a golden signet ring, the huge large ruby etched with a flaming dragon's wing. "I'm guessing this looks familiar to you?" Mateo inquired.

"You know it does," Alaric stepped forward, looking closely at the ring, noting the smaller band and intricate scrollwork. It was my grandmother's. "As far as I knew it was lost when she was beheaded by the bloody Duke of Argyll in the Battle of Sheriffmuir." His brogue grew thicker with every word. "I had come to the New World five years earlier. Settled with the Spanish down south, where San Antonio now sits. It took nearly four months for Androu's letter to arrive. There was nothing left of our homestead. The bastards took what they could pillage and burned the rest." He took a long, deep drink, attempting to let the warm amber liquid calm his nerves. "But you know that I'm sure. I can't imagine Clarence Collins letting his most prized pupil out on his first solo mission without all the facts. Don't you guys have like a Hall of Records or a Supercomputer or something to keep every scrap of information and intimate detail of us Supers hidden away in your secret compound somewhere?"

"Indeed," was Mateo's only response as he once again swiped his fingers across the screen of his phone.

Opening his mouth to ask the asshole to get on with it before he ripped his heart out, Alaric waited instead as the sound of ringing proceeded the icy calm voice of none other than Clarence Collins, the Directive's legendary Enforcer, and all-around total bastard. "Hello, Alaric. How are you doing this evening?"

Once again, he was forced to bite his tongue as his mind was invaded for no other reason than the Clarence the Bastard liked to flex his muscle. The battle between them had been waging for centuries, and Alaric was in no mood to go another round. Plastering on his usual cocky grin, he replied, "Doing well, Old Man. And you?"

Ignoring his question, never answering any questions unless forced, always the one to do the asking, the Enforcer went on as if Alaric hadn't spoken. "What do you make of the photo? Is that not the insignia of your family, of Clan MacAngoran?"

"Aye. It is the crest given to my mother's family, and worn by any, and all my grandmother and her companion Androu, brought into the family."

"And you have yours?"

Raising his hand, the thought of flipping Mateo off making him smile, Alaric wiggled the fingers on his right hand, dropping it back to his side as the younger Enforcer replied, "He has it on."

"Do you know who the one in the photo belongs to?"

Clarence's tone was steely. The bastard was driving at something, and Alaric wasn't answering another fucking question until someone told him what was going on and preferably in the next five seconds. He could feel the Dragon fire, a gift from Carrick upon the completion of their Bond of Brotherhood, racing through his veins. Tapping his fingers together, he growled low in his throat as sparks danced in the air around him.

"What exactly are you driving at?" Alaric demanded.

"Who does the ring belong to?" Clarence reiterated, his voice lower, his power making the silver device in Mateo's hand vibrate.

Changing tactics, Alaric spoke just barely above a whisper and asked, "Where did you find it?" Giving another snap of his fingers to remind the Enforcer before him who he was dealing with, Alaric smirked.

Silence, as cold as the grave and infinitely more deadly, stretched between them. Alaric knew he was poking the bear, the bear that could sentence him to death with the blink of an eye and damn it all if it didn't feel good. He was sick and tired of being fucked with, and this was where he was taking his stand.

Staring at Mateo because Clarence hadn't deemed it necessary to travel, Alaric refused to be intimidated by the likes of the Enforcer's lackey. They would fucking answer his questions or get the hell out of his club.

Giving a single nod, obviously telepathically conspiring with his boss, Mateo reached forward, pressed a button on his phone, glaring at Alaric as the gruesome photo of a bloody crime scene popped into view. Stepping closer, he saw the open cavity of what used to be a woman's neck, the skin shredded down the length of both her arms revealing bone and muscle that had been gnawed on by long, sharp canines and the bite marks between her legs and covering her sex.

Blinking as the picture changed, he fought to keep down the bile rising in his throat as a close-up shot showed his grandmother's ring sitting on the dead woman's left ring finger. Grabbing the phone from Mateo, ignoring the Enforcer's warning snarl, the ancient Vampire flipped through all the photos, looking for any clue as to the identity of the perpetrator of this heinous crime.

There it was, in the last picture, barely visible except with his preternatural sight. Dropping the device into Mateo's outstretched hand, Alaric walked around his desk, casually taking a seat when he felt like falling. Pointing towards the Enforcer before him while speaking directly to Clarence, Alaric challenged, "You saw it, didn't you? You spotted the small ribbon of tartan tied around the hem of the woman's dress and straightaway sent your attack dog to question me?"

"Yes." The Enforcer's one-word answer dropped like a live grenade between Alaric and Mateo. Long seconds ticked by until Clarence finally added, "I saw the tartan. I know it is from Clan MacAngoran. I further know that your grandmother, Brygid and her consort, Androu, made that the colors of their Clan of Vampires just about the time you were Made."

Knowing there was more to come, Alaric drained his glass and slammed it onto the mahogany top of his eighteenth-century Governor's desk. Pulling open the bottom desk drawer, he lifted out a new bottle of Macallan 25, cracked the seal, refilled his glass and downed it as Clarence began again.

"I also know that you have been nowhere near San Antonio, specifically the site of The Alamo in the last thirty days." Clearing his throat, the Enforcer spoke to his protégée, "Show him the other photos, Mateo."

Drinking another two fingers of Scotch, Alaric grabbed Mateo's phone as it slid across the desktop and thumbed through eleven more photos of six more victims. Each brutally drained, half-eaten, then left with a signet ring from the MacAngoran Clan and a ribbon of tartan.

Sitting back in his chair, Alaric finally answered the Enforcer's initial question, "The first ring belonged to Brygid. It is one of a kind, matches mine and was given to us by the Leader of the Dragons when our bond was forged."

"And the others?"

"You mean for those later turned?"

"Yes." Again, Clarence's one-word answer grated on Alaric's frayed nerves, but he knew answering was the quickest way to get rid of the asshole.

"They had simple gold bands, very little scrollwork, smaller rubies, all etched with the flaming dragon wings."

"And the ones in the photographs, where did they come from?"

"I have no clue. They look newer. The bands are plain like I said," he ground out. "Even the older rings had some scrollwork, it was the one thing besides the etched ruby that Brygid demanded." He ran his fingers through his hair. "There are only four of us left from what she called the *Ceannródaí* or Pioneers. Have you found the others?"

"We are looking." Clarence's voice actually held the slightest touch of what Alaric thought might have been empathy, but then he spoke again, and all that remained was the steely resolve to find the rogue Vampire running around Texas on a murder spree. "There's one more thing you need to know."

"And what might that be?" Alaric grumbled, taking a drink straight from the bottle.

"There is something I left out of the photos, the last piece of the puzzle that assures me it is either one of the remaining MacAngoran Vampires or someone trying to frame you and yours by killing humans and leaving their bodies out in the open."

"Go on, Mr. Wizard, tell me. I can't think of anything more damning than the tartan."

"What about white roses with their thorns removed? Ring any bells?"

"Son of a bitch, I will decapitate the bastard myself," Alaric roared, throwing his glass against the far wall before storming out of the office.

6

———

eturning to her seat, having more fun than she'd ever expected, Ashlynn took a long drink of her iced, disguised as beer in a Corona bottle compliments of Sampson, as Leslie came bouncing her way giggling like a schoolgirl. "Damn Ash, I didn't think you had it in you. Getting spanked by a Dom in a leather mask? What will the other doctors say?"

"Who gives a shit? It's a party," she whooped, drinking what was left of her tea before slamming the empty bottle down on the table and laughing, "So, tell me Dr. Party Pants, how am I doin'?"

"I'm givin' you an A for attitude with a positive outlook for a clean sweep on the rest of the night."

"Have you been able to persuade tall, dark and hooded hottie to go home with you yet?" Ashlynn asked, having witnessed her friend's dogged pursuit of a certain Dom with smoky grey eyes and a tattoo of a black panther covering the left side of his chest.

"I'm wearing him down, Ash. Ya' know what they say, the best part of getting the guy is the chase." Leslie laughed out loud, setting her empty glass on the table alongside her others. "And girl, I'm havin' a damn fine time."

"Get 'em, Les," the young doctor hollered at her friend's back as the phone in her back pocket began to vibrate.

Pulling the red-and-white-heart-covered device from her pocket, Ash immediately read '911' on the screen and headed for the door. Typing and sending her response as she went. 'On the way. ETA 15 minutes.'

Reaching for the knob, her hand collided with another much larger, much colder one. Looking up, ready to yell at whoever was in her way, Ash tried to remain calm as her eyes met Sampson's. Holding up her phone, she explained, "Gotta go. One of my patients just took a turn for the worst."

"Oh shit," he responded. "Do your friends know?"

Feeling horrible that she hadn't thought about Leslie, Cecily or the others, Ashlynn shook her head and started to turn, but Sampson's free hand on her shoulder stopped her in her tracks as he spoke into his headset, "Hey Axel, when this part of the act dies down and the ladies are waiting for the last set of guys, can you tell Leslie and Cecily that Ashlynn had an emergency at the hospital."

There was a second of silence before Sampson nodded, "Will do, Brother. Thank you." Wrapping the hand that had been on her shoulder around her hand, he opened the door with the other and pulled her along, calling over his shoulder, "Come on, I'll get you out of here as quick as I can."

Jogging to keep up with the long strides of the man she would always think of as 'the Viking', Ashlynn typed, 'Need vitals' on her phone and hit send as they traveled down one hall, made a left, and headed towards the soft, sensual music of the dancefloor at the front of the club.

Stopping just short of running into Sampson's back as she was reading the message on her phone, Ash pushed up onto her toes and with her mouth close to his ear asked, "What's the holdup?"

Turning to the side, she saw the frown on Sampson's face as he gruffly replied, "Looks like Security's breaking up some kind of scuffle. Thankfully it doesn't happen very often. Mostly because if you cause any kind of disturbance you're banned for life and Alaric, the owner, has a really long memory."

"Is there any other way out? I hate to be a pain in the ass, but I need to get to Children's Medical Center down off Harry Hines Blvd as soon as possible."

Without answering, the Viking touched the button on his headset and ordered, "Get me a taxi. Have them out front and ready to roll in two minutes. Tell them there's a hundred-dollar tip in it for them if they can get the fares to Children's Medical in ten minutes."

Astounded that a man she'd just met, a vampire to boot, would help her in such a way, filled Ashlynn with hope. Her mom had always said she should look for signs of faith at work, and that when she found them, it meant there were more to come. Ash could only pray her mom had been right and that the good fortune she was having would spread over to her patient.

"Hold on," was the only warning she got before Sampson lifted her feet off the floor, placed her over his shoulder and in a loud booming voice announced, "Outta the way people. Make a path. Injured guest needs medical attention. Make a path. Make a damn path, will ya'?"

Not putting up a fuss because he was getting her through the crowd, Ash still couldn't help being embarrassed that her butt was in the air while being carried out of the hottest nightclub in Dallas by a really good-looking Vampire. Keeping her eyes closed tight, not wanting to ogle her new friend's backside, she knew the second they'd crossed over onto the dancefloor when the clomp of the heels of Sampson's boots could be heard over the loud music.

Praying to God, no one recognized her or rather her ass, what Sampson had said before throwing her over his shoulder finally registered in her otherwise occupied brain. So, it was true. Alaric, the elusive millionaire or billionaire or insanely rich man, however, someone described him in one of the many articles written about him, *was* a Vampire. She guessed that explained his elusive nature and the mystical look he exuded in every photograph she'd ever seen. It was probably easier to stay out of the limelight whenever possible, even though Vampires had been 'out of the coffin' for years.

They were blamed for any and every crime committed, at least in Dallas, Houston and San Antonio where she had hospital privileges and tended to be. It really was a shame that Vampires were treated so badly after admitting that they truly did exist. She'd always been of the opinion that if they felt more comfortable, maybe some would come forward and consent to have their blood studied. Who knew, maybe there was something in there that could be synthesized to help others of their kind, as well as humans. But as it was, she knew there was a real danger of them becoming little more than lab rats to some overzealous, megalomaniac hell-bent on world domination.

Pulled from her thoughts as Sampson put her feet on the floor and turned her towards the door, Ashlynn spoke over her shoulder as she rushed to the waiting cab. "Thank you so very much, Sampson. You've been a lifesaver. I owe you lunch or coffee."

"No problem, anyt..."

"Sampson!" The roar came from somewhere behind them cutting off whatever the Viking was about to say. "Sampson! Stop! Now! Get her back here." The voice continued as Ash jumped into the cab and Sampson slammed the door, pounding on the trunk of the bright yellow vehicle as a signal for the driver to go.

Squealing away from the curb, driving well over the speed limit, Ash reached for her seatbelt and took a glance out the back window, wanting to at least mouth another 'Thank you' to Sampson. What she saw had her turning completely around and getting on her knees to make sure her eyes weren't deceiving her.

There, in the middle of the street, was Sampson holding back an obviously pissed off Alaric, aka, sexy club owner. Trying to look more closely as the taxi sped away, Ashlynn attempted to read the Vampire's lips, but sadly, she was too far away.

Taking her seat and buckling her belt after nearly being thrown onto the floor when the cab driver took a corner on two wheels, Ashlynn forgot about whatever was happening at *CRAVE* as her phone once again alerted her to another text message. Reading the words, 'Prepping for Surgery. Stent is malfunctioning.', she could only pray that she got there in time. Her only priority at the moment was saving Timmy James, not a night out with friends, not a new friend, not even a millionaire Vampire she almost got to meet.

"Life and death never takes a break. Hold on Timmy, I'm coming."

7

___

"Get your fucking hands off of me," Alaric roared, slamming his fist into Sampson's jaw. "Who the fuck do you think you are?" He swung again at the shocked Viking he'd known for centuries. Only hitting air as Sampson took a step to the right, the momentum spun him completely around, to find a glaring Ruari at his back.

"Calm down, Boss," his Second whispered in warning, signaling over his shoulder with a slide of his eyes. "You and Sam need to be careful. Someone might think you're doin' more than messin' around."

"Yeah, Alaric, I thought we were due for training tomorrow," Sampson joked, helping with the façade Ruari was creating. "I get that you want to sharpen your street-fighting technique, but damn, surprise attacks don't come til later."

What the hell is wrong with me? I'm losing my mind. Sniffing the air and looking over his shoulder, it took all of his hard-fought control not to run after the woman who smelled like poppies and buttercups and had a voice like an angel.

I have to know who she is. I have to have her...possess her... she is mine...

Vibrating with rage, ignoring Mateo as the Enforcer stood nearly ten feet back with his arms crossed over his chest and his feet shoulder width apart, Alaric did an about-face and stalked away, calling telepathically to Ruari, *"Meet me in the Galley. Bring Sampson."*

Turning abruptly into the alley running between *CRAVE* and the empty building that used to be a seafood restaurant called *The Galley,* Alaric scented the air, holding tightly to the lingering scent of the flowers of his homeland, trying to conjure up what the woman who'd been thrown over Sampson's shoulder truly looked like.

Punching in the code on the electronic keypad, he entered the building he'd bought and refurbished for more than just extra offices for his staff and went straight to the back. Opening the three-and-a-half-foot thick steel door that led to the twenty-five by twenty-foot vault he'd had installed, he went straight to the refrigerator, took out three bags of blood and tried to quench his thirst before the others arrived.

Images of his daydreams infiltrated his mind. The woman he'd seen with Sampson had the same silken curls, the same glorious smile, mesmerizingly chocolate brown eyes and the most erotically devastating curves he'd ever witnessed.

"And I want to rip that fucking Viking's throat out for ever touching her," he growled.

Downing all three bags of the crimson liquid in minutes, nearly gagging on the cold, stale, stagnant, utterly insipid flavor of what had sustained him for so many centuries, Alaric disposed of the empty bags as he heard the approach of the others. Not surprised to see Mateo in attendance, he calmly asked, "What can I do for you? I was under the impression our business was suspended until you have further information for me."

Smirking like a Cheshire cat, the newest Enforcer scoffed, "The shattered crystal on your office floor and the vanishing bruise on Sampson's chin say otherwise." Stepping forward, he narrowed his eyes. "Wanna tell me what's going on with you?"

Shrugging as he sat on the edge of the cherry wood desk and crossed his ankles, Alaric opened his arms wide. "Nothing I'm aware of." Holding onto the growling, seething beast within his soul, squelching the flames threatening to burst forth from his fingertips, he added with a wink and an exaggerated southern twang that sounded all the funnier combined with his Scottish brogue. "Business as usual here in the Big D, Sir."

Adding a mock salute at the end, sure he'd taken things one step too far for the uptight, obviously-trying-to-impress-his-boss Enforcer, Alaric prepared to defend his actions when Mateo snatched his phone from the inside pocket of his jacket. Holding up the index finger of his free hand, Mateo answered the call.

"Bianchi here."

Silence filled the vault as the deep voice of Clarence Collins filled the room even though the call was not on speakerphone. "There is another body. Dragon Park, a small privately-owned reserve on the north side of Dallas."

"Same as the others?"

"Worse." Clarence cleared his throat. "This one is missing its head and hands, and..." There was a pause in which Alaric could hear the ancient Enforcer speaking to another. When he returned, his voice was laced with a rage Clarence usually kept within his iron grip. "It was just confirmed that the woman is Vampire. Young, only a few hundred years old. Still unable to stand daylight and easily subdued by one older and stronger. Is Alaric there?"

"Aye, I'm here."

"This one has a message I am assuming is for you." Clarence's voice held more than a little accusation.

Gripping the edge of the desk with such force he could feel the wood splintering within his grasp, Alaric coaxed, "Let's have it then. Donnae leave me hangin'." At the sound of his brogue deepening, a sure sign his anger was getting the best of him, Ruari's head jerked to the side, his raised eyebrow and deepening frown showing the Vampire's concern for his boss.

Shaking his head to calm his friend, it was Alaric who needed to be settled as Clarence continued, "The message, *A thabhairt duit, Deartháir* is written in the victim's blood on the stone base of the brass statue of the Archangel Gabriel."

Taking a deep breath then slowly letting it out, Alaric focused on Clarence's words as he thought of the only other person in all the world who would taunt him with the words, 'To you, Brother.' The sound of the legendary Enforcer clearing his throat pulled Alaric from his thoughts. "Since Mateo has been with you all evening and this murder happened no more than two hours ago, we now have concrete proof that you are not involved."

"Thank you for that," Alaric grumbled, still trying to keep both his rage and his Dragon fire under control as Sampson asked, "For those of us who don't speak Gaelic, what the hell is going on?

"Would you like to field this one, Alaric?" Clarence asked, but it was Ruari who answered, giving a single nod to his boss.

"It's an old threat. One that was left in the villages that

were plundered by the Celtic traitors who sided with the Romans during the Cimbrian War." He cleared his throat, obviously remembering the carnage from his youth. "The fuckin' assholes would take the blood of the children and write, 'To you, Brother' to taunt the Celts still fighting to protect our lands on the Jutland Peninsula."

"And you have an idea who this is?" Clarence's direct question and unrelenting tone left no room to hedge. He wanted answers, and he wanted them now.

"I do. Although there are only four of us left from the MacAngoran Clan, there are many others of other Covens and Clans who were alive during that time and who fought for both sides. Give me twenty-four hours. Ruari and I will find out what bastard from our past is in the city."

"You need not get involved." Clarence was giving a direct order, one that crawled up Alaric's spine and made his beast roar for battle. "Mateo will..."

"Will go about his job and I shall go about mine," Alaric responded, letting the tiniest bit of his power flow towards the Enforcer-in-Training and therefore, his boss as well.

Deafening silence filled the room. Alaric felt the push of Clarence's power, still incredibly formidable although his only connection was through the airwaves. When the Enforcer spoke, it was saturated with utter control and absolute power. "Do not interfere with our investigation, Alaric. Share everything you learn with Mateo as you learn it, *not* a second later." His threat was clear, you hide anything from me, you die. It was as simple as that. The Directive didn't play, they didn't ask twice, and they *did* exterminate with extreme prejudice.

"Aye, Clarence."

The words were barely out of his mouth before Mateo disconnected the call, stowed his phone back inside his jacket and looked directly at Alaric. "I'll be back." Without another word, the Enforcer-in-Training turned and left, nearly disappearing into thin air with the use of his preternatural speed.

Barking with laughter, Ruari held his stomach as he guffawed, "Does that joker really think he's Schwarzenegger?"

"I'll be back," Sampson mocked, getting in on the joke, imitating the well-known Austrian-American actor's unmistakable accent. "Dude better lay off the Terminator."

Unable to keep the smile from spreading across his face, Alaric strolled to the bar, poured three glasses of blood-laced port, picked his up and turned towards his still chuckling friends. Watching Ruari and Sampson, the ancient vampire tried to mentally focus on the two people of his Clan still walking the earth. Being a blood relative of Brygid, the Sire of Clan MacAngoran, he could touch the mind of every Vampire with her blood running through their veins.

Quickly locating Thaddeus, the vampire who was still trying, all these centuries later, to atone for his actions as a young vampire, kneeling at the altar of St Moluag's in Lismore in the county of Argyll, Alaric took an extra second to prepare to speak with his brethren.

Dressed in the heavy, dark brown, woolen robes of the holy men of the third century B.C., his long red hair pulled back and held at the nape of his neck with a leather wrap, the ancient Vampire's prayers of redemption and penance touched Alaric's heart. It had been so long since they'd spoken that he'd forgotten how oppressive his brethren's guilt was.

"Thaddeus, brother, how are ye?" He spoke directly into the other Vampire's mind. *"Will you never accept the forgiveness I know you been granted time and again?"*

"I seek not the mercy from our Lord, but from my own soul, of this you well know, Brother."

And Alaric did. He had been there when Androu had brought a sobbing Thaddeus into the MacAngoran Castle. Crazed with hunger, refusing to feed, the newly turned Vampire's mind had forsaken him. On the fifth night, the need to feed or perish came over Thad with the force of the devil himself. The young man jumped from the turret, some seventy-five feet atop the west side of the castle, raced into the village and drained nearly ten people before Alaric was able to stop him.

Easily overpowering the young vampire, Alaric carried Thad back to the castle, locked him in the dungeon and spent the next hundred years keeping him alive with cow's blood hidden in his food and drink. Thaddeus had never again taken food from a human neck. It was a tragic tale of what can come from turning the unwilling.

"Aye, Thaddeus, someday you must find the way to forgive yourself. Live the life you have been given."

"You have not reached across the multitude of miles separating us to reiterate the words you have spoken for centuries," Thaddeus sighed, still on his knees, head bent, hands on the elegantly carved wood altar rail. *"Ask what you need to ask and let me be."*

"As you wish." Alaric hated that thousands of years later a man he thought of as a brother still suffered so, but there was more at stake than Thaddeus' penance. That had been going on for several lifetimes and would have to wait.

"Have you spoken to Androu?"

"No, not since the day I left that dreadful place, and I pray to our gracious Lord that I never do."

Ignoring the depths of his own regret for the part he played in keeping Thad locked in the dungeon for all those years, Alaric asked his last question. *"Have you seen any of the others? Any of our kind or any from the Clans or Covens? Any from the time of the Roman Invasion?"*

"No, I have not." Thaddeus' disgust for all things Vampire was palpable. *"As you well know, you are the only one of our kind that I have any correspondence with, all others are banned from my mind, as well as this holy place."*

Sorry for the toll his questions had taken on his brother, Alaric apologized, *"Excuse my interruption of your prayers. Be well, Brother."*

"You as well, Alaric."

The carefully constructed, incredibly strong walls within Thaddeus' mind slammed shut just as Sampson, who had moved while Alaric was otherwise engaged, clapped his hands and teased, "Wake up, Sleepyhead. We've got business to attend to."

Looking the tall Nordic Vampire directly in the eye, Alaric narrowed his eyes and nodded, "Indeed, we do. Tell me everything you know about the woman I saw you manhandling, starting with her name and leaving nothing out, lest you feel like losing your head on this night."

Jumping out of the cab, Ashlynn ran through the huge, double, automatic, glass doors of the Emergency entrance of Children's Medical, made an immediate left and sprinted for the stairs at the end of the hall. Crashing through the door, she hit the stairs like she'd been shot out of a cannon, before taking the steps three at a time and landing on the painted concrete floor of the basement in record time.

Speeding towards the Surgical Suite, she was met by Tracy and Angela, the two nurse practitioners who were part of her surgical team. Hitting the double doors leading to the Scrub Room with her back, Ashlynn spun towards the huge, deep, stainless steel sinks and began scrubbing in as one nurse helped her out of her clothes and into scrubs while the other gave her vital information on her patient.

"BP is Sixty-seven over thirty-two, hemoglobin at four and white count at fourteen-point-six as of fifteen minutes ago."

The emotion in Angela's voice was controlled, but nonetheless still there. It was no secret that they'd all gotten close to Timmy. He was a good kid who'd been dealt a raw deal by genetics, Fate, Destiny or whatever bastard was responsible for kids with bad hearts and rare blood types.

"Our boy's got an infection," Ash commented, unconsciously scrubbing her skin so hard her skin turned bright red. Pulling her hands from the water and bending her elbows upright so Tracy could slide the surgical gown onto her body, Ashlynn continued, "Liver functions, creatinine, and A1C are off the charts?"

"They are," Angela confirmed before Tracy added, "And his fluid retention is damn near more than an adult three times his size," while stuffing Ashlynn's long, light-brown braid into her pink, flowered surgical cap and tying it tightly at the base of the surgeon's neck along with the strings to her surgical mask. Covering Ashlynn's mouth with the thick cotton-like fabric, the nurse tied the second set of strings atop the crown of the young surgeon's head and confirmed, "The shield for your eyes is on your tray next to your light and scope."

"Thanks, Trace." Ash took her first deep breath since racing into the hospital and calmed the twinge of nerves she always felt right before surgery. At first, those uneasy feelings had worried her, made her think she wasn't cut out to be a surgeon, but Dr. Higgenbotham, her professor, and mentor, was quick to reassure a then resident praying with words she still repeated before every procedure. *Nerves are good. They remind you that you are human. That you are about to hold another human's life in your hands. As long as you have a conscience, you have a soul, and therefore, respect the sanctity of life. You, Ashlynn, will always give all that you have to your patients. Never fear the nerves, embrace them, let them fuel your desire to preserve the life you have sworn to protect. You are one of the good ones, Kiddo. Make me proud."*

I plan to do just that, Dr. H. Wherever in Heaven you may be, I thank you.

"He's in multi-system failure. Get ready ladies, we're about to replace the stent, hook him up with a pacemaker, and give our boy a few more weeks, so, we can find him a new heart."

"We're right behind you," the nurses answered in unison as Ashlynn once again used her back to open another set of doors. Turning, she looked at her patient, so young, frail and very much in danger of losing his life.

Glancing up at Dr. Williams, the anesthesiologist Ash most liked to work with, she nodded, "You got our boy good and asleep?"

"He's ready for your magic, Doc."

Giving the other doctor a wink and grinning even though she felt anything but jovial, Ash looked at the entire surgical team and shoving as much positive energy and good vibes into her voice as she could, instructed, "This one's for all the marbles. Prayers, good thoughts, and healing energy along with everything Dr. Simmons and I can do is what's gonna save Timmy. Thank you for being here. Let's get to work."

Stepping up to the table supporting her young patient, Ashlynn's eyes met Bob Simmons', the assisting thoracic surgeon, and in unison, they gave each other a single nod before getting to work. Nine-and-a-half long, soul-sucking, energy-draining hours they worked to replace the stent on the anterior cardiac artery, place a new one on the posterior side and also implant a pacemaker to keep the boy's heart beating at a regular, healthy rhythm.

During the long, treacherous procedure, Timmy went into cardiac arrest twice, had to be given ten pints of blood – which meant he lost not only the eight pints he'd come into surgery with, but also two additional units- and was on the razor's edge of death more times than Ashlynn wanted to think about. Staying until Dr. Simmons had the boy's chest closed and the nurses were taking him to recovery, the young surgeon held her head high, got out of her bloody clothes, changed into a new set of scrubs and headed out to talk to his parents.

Walking into the waiting room, she was immediately met by Mr. and Mrs. James, along with Timmy's grandparents, two aunts, and an uncle. Motioning for them to sit back down, Ash pulled up a chair and sat in front of the semi-circle the family had formed while waiting.

Smiling at each person as she spoke, Ash assured them, "Timmy did a fantastic job. He's a real fighter, super strong, you should be proud." Taking Mrs. James' hand as the mother with red-rimmed eyes and cheer-stained cheeks reached for her, Ashlynn continued, "You know that I'm always honest with you, so, here goes. Tim's heart did stop twice, he did lose a lot of blood, and he's still not out of the woods." She watched as everyone held their breath waiting for the good news and hurried on. "All of that being said, he rallied back and held tight as we put in two stents and a pacemaker. He will be on daily dialysis until he's off the ventilator as a precaution. We need to be sure he doesn't retain any more fluids than absolutely necessary. We do not want his heart working any harder than it has to." She squeezed Mrs. James' hand and smiled at Mr. James. "I will be calling Houston, San Antonio, Seattle, Baltimore, and D.C. as soon as I can get to a phone and speak with the heads of their Transplant Units to see if they have any information on an AB negative match for Timmy."

Letting go of Mrs. James' hand, Ash stood and made her way around to each relative, shaking their hands as she concluded, "I'll be here until he wakes up. Tracy and Angela are with him in recovery, as well as, Barbara and Kristine, so, y'all know he's in the best hands we've got." Winking as she pointed at the coffee pot, she added, "I'll call Culinary and have them come up with some brunch and drinks."

"Thank you so much," Mr. James' low, Texas drawl rang out right before the entire family echoed his appreciation. "If anyone can help our boy, it's you, Dr. Ash."

Holding back the tears, Ashlynn smiled and nodded, "I'm sure gonna give it my best."

Walking out of the room, still maintaining her air of confidence, she made it into the elevator, up to the tenth floor and into the Chapel before letting her tears of sadness, fear, exhaustion, and utter confusion at a world where a boy like Timmy could suffer so much, fall. Glad the Sanctuary was empty, she slowly made her way to the front pew. Sitting on the end closest to the far wall, under the shroud of shadows caused by the glow of the electric candles perched in the golden candelabras, Ashlynn talked to God.

"I know you were in the Operating Room with us. I could feel your guidance with every cut, every decision, every step of the way. I have asked a lot of you over the years, probably more than I had a right to, but I have to ask more. Please, if it is your will, help me help Timmy. Whatever way that may be, in whatever form you deem necessary, I am asking you to be with that amazing little boy and not let his suffering be in vain."

Unable to speak as her sobs continued to grow, Ashlynn continued her plea silently, letting go of her need to control and fix in favor of the Higher Power she knew with all her heart would lead her to the answers she needed to make sure Timmy had a long, healthy life. Thinking of her mom and dad and grandma Judy, she thought of all the times they'd prayed together as a family for one of her dad's patients or her mother's clients. Growing up with a father who was also a surgeon, a mother who was a social worker and a grandmother who was a retired nurse, all who had a strong faith in not only God but also in the inherent goodness of people, Ashlynn truly believed everything happened the way it was supposed to in its own time – and Timmy's situation was no different.

It was almost as if she could hear her father's voice reassuring, *"You've done all you can, Doodlebug. You gave it you're all. The rest is up to God. Believe, and your answers will come."*

"I do, Daddy. I believe so much it hurts. I know with my heart and soul that Timmy is destined for great things. I just have to help him make it there."

Waiting for the reply she knew wasn't coming, Ashlynn jumped to her feet when a voice called out over the loudspeaker, "Code Blue Recovery. Code Blue Recovery. Code Blue Recovery."

Racing out of the chapel, she collided with a tall, handsome man whose hands gently closed on her upper arms as he kept her from hitting the floor. Icy hot goose bumps rose on her flesh. Her own heart skipped a beat, and the air was forced from her lungs.

Looking into his gunmetal-blue eyes, she felt something weird happen in the deep recesses of her soul. She couldn't shake the feeling that she knew him from somewhere or the way one look made her want to jump into his arms and never leave.

Not able or willing to examine what was going on as the

terrifying words 'Code Blue' continued through the halls, Ash exclaimed, "Sorry. Thank you. So Sorry."

Racing towards Recovery, terrified at what she might find, for a split-second her steps faltered as the words, *"My pleasure, Ashlynn. We shall meet again,"* floated through her mind.

9

Watching Ashlynn sprint down the hall and not chasing after her took every ounce of control in Alaric's body and soul. The tips of his fangs drew blood from his bottom lip. His nails, now claws, bit into his flesh. Sparks, quickly growing into small flames, danced in his palms, and skated over his wrists before he could force it down. A red haze eclipsed his vision. Searing pain, the twisting of his muscles, the cramping of his stomach, the throbbing of his cock, nearly forced the vampire to his knees.

Thinking about what Sampson had told him just a few hours earlier, Alaric let the conversation replay in his mind, praying it would dampen the need roaring within him...

"And when did you meet her?" Alaric demanded his tone deep and threatening.

"Whoa, chill, Al," Ruari stepped up to his side. "Sam is here for the bachelorette party I told you about. The one where the groom is a friend of Roarke's and requested extra security?"

At the mention of his fellow vampire's name, Alaric asked,

"And Roarke knows of this woman?" Stepping forward, he snarled, "She is not one of his thirty-day girls, is she?"

"I'm not sure if Roarke knows Ash and let me assure you with a big ole HELL NO, she is not from the Service," Sampson answered, taking up where Ruari had left off. "All I know is that Ashlynn knows Roarke's wife, Katharine, and also Remy Newman's wife, Bonnie. They went to the same high school or something like that. They didn't sound like close friends, but she smiled when she talked about them, so, I guess they are still on good terms."

Hearing Ashlynn's name, Alaric instinctually took another step forward, growling through gritted teeth, "Exactly how close did you get to Ashlynn? You seem to know more than you are saying." Poking the tall Nordic vampire in the chest, Alaric accused, "She is mine. I will have her, and no one will stop me. If you have so much as left a fingerprint on her person, I will make your death slow and painful."

Holding his hands up, palms out, showing his surrender, Sampson shook his head, "Dude, take a breath. I don't want her for anything more than a friend. She is super smart, really easy to talk to and very nice." With his hands still up but now grinning, he added, "She's a heart surgeon for kids. Like one of the best in the whole world." His awe was evident in the way his eyes danced, and the excitement lifted in his baritone voice. Pulling out his phone, quickly sliding his fingers over the screen, he handed the device to Alaric. "Look at that shit. That's Ashlynn's bio in Who's Who in Medicine." Shaking his head and chuckling, the Viking added, "Not only is she brilliant, but she's also the youngest female to ever be at the top of her field in Cardiothoracic and Cardiovascular Surgery. It's amazing. She is a rock star in her field." He whistled through his teeth. "And she knew I was a Vampire, just from looking. Gave me all the signs then said it was because of her training. I thought it was cool as shit."

"And she wasn't apprehensive or scared?" Ruari asked. "She didn't think you were gonna overpower her, drag her into a dark corner and drain her."

"Hell no," Sampson laughed. "She was totally cool. Interested in what makes us the way we are, but totally respectful and shit. I'm tellin' ya' Ru, Ashlynn is cool people."

Wholeheartedly agreeing but keeping his thoughts to himself, Alaric couldn't look away from the smiling photo of the most beautiful woman he'd ever seen. Just the sight of her made him recall how one whiff of her succulent scent had driven him wild. The need to have her, hold her, be with her was overwhelming. Had cut through his devastating hunger, given him the purpose and direction he'd been without since that first horrifying nightmare over thirty days ago.

"You will never touch her again. Do you understand?" Alaric grumbled, adding power to his voice so that there was no mistaking his position on the matter.

"Yeah, sure. Whatever you say. I only carried her out of the club because that asshole was causing trouble in Silk Fantasies and the Lookie Loos were blocking every fuckin' hallway. I thought I was helping."

"I'm sure you did...help." Throwing Sampson's phone back to him, Alaric turned on the heel of his boot, dashed out of the vault and ran through the streets at top speed, only stopping when he was inside the hospital. Scouring the halls, he quickly found her scent, then waited in awe as he watched how tenderly and compassionately she comforted her patient's parents.

Following closely when she left the waiting room, he'd felt her sadness, known she needed time alone and had respected that as far as he could. Racing up the stairs, keeping up with the quickly rising elevator, he'd exited the stairwell just a few steps behind her. Waiting until she was in the Chapel, he'd slipped into the *back, stood against the wall and watched until the loudspeaker had interrupted Ashlynn's prayers.*

That was where Alaric had lost his battle. His need to know her had been the victor. He'd had to touch her, to speak to her, to make any connection that he could, no matter how brief.

Inhaling deeply, the scent of buttercups and poppies wrapping around him, through him, over him, a balm to his soul and relief to his agony, Alaric panted. His fangs retracted. His claws reverted to his usual well-manicured nails, and his pain floated away, taking with it the hunger, if only for a few moments. Unfortunately, the insatiable desire to have Ashlynn by his side, within his arms, her beautiful body accepting his over and over again, pushed his erection past pleasure to pain as it threatened to rip through the zipper of his pants.

Stumbling into the Chapel, Alaric dropped into the first pew he came to, hidden by the darkness and shadows. There had to be something incredibly wrong with a Vampire being in a Sanctuary, with a hard-on, unable to control his dark urges for more than a few minutes, but it couldn't be helped. Gods forgive him, dreams of his cock buried deep inside Ashlynn, her nails scoring his back, her screams of pleasure feeding their mutual desire were running through his mind like horses around a track.

"Son of a b..." He swallowed the curse, sure he was already damned to Hell, but not wanting a ticket on the Express Train. "My epitaph will read 'Doomed".

Churches, religion...his faith, they'd all been very important to him before he became a vampire, and had been one of the few things that had seen him through learning to control his hunger and living without the sun. He'd even fallen to his knees and praised the Heavens the day he'd returned to the light and walked under the shining rays of the sun.

Over the years, as the world became more learned, so did he and so did his beliefs. It was something private and personal, not something he shared with anyone...but Thaddeus.

Looking at the altar, his eyes lit on the cross. Once again, his mind was drawn to Thad. Without overthinking it, he called to his brethren for the second time in less than twenty-four hours. Something that hadn't happened for nearly four hundred years.

Poking at the mental blocks his brother-in-arms had constructed, Alaric finally broke through and called out, *"Thaddeus, please do not deny me your wisdom. I fear I'm losing my mind, and am in need of your counsel."*

The cold, austere silence was almost as frightening as the madness closing in all around him. His control slipping a little more with every passing heartbeat, Alaric gripped the hard, wooden armrest, trying his best not to rip it from the back. There was no way he would lose control, no way he would go rogue. He was a Super. He'd lived more than two millennia. There was no way in Heaven or Hell he was letting himself fall into the darkness, only to be hunted by the likes of Clarence Collins and his band of bloodthirsty Enforcers. If Thaddeus wouldn't help him, then he'd find someone else. There was simply no...

"Quiet your mind, Brother. I am here." Thaddeus' words broke through the cacophony of chaos, throwing out a bright, glowing lifeline that Alaric gripped with both hands.

"Thank the gods you answered. It's happening. What you predicted all those years ago. I am finally losing my mind, Brother. The icy claws of madness have taken hold. I feel my sanity slipping away."

"Tell me of your experience. I am sure that together we can see you through to the other side of whatever ails you."

A wave of warm, uplifting calm followed Thaddeus' words, allowing Alaric to put his thoughts in order. Once again, as it always was when he spoke to Thaddeus, guilt over their shared past rose up within the ancient Vamp, remorse that he somehow knew would follow him for all his days.

Shaking it off, Alaric began to explain, *"It started with a dream over a month ago. I saw bodies everywhere. Their throats torn out, severed limbs lying in piles, the walls painted in blood."* He paused, preparing to utter the words he hadn't shared with anyone, not even Ruari, when Thaddeus whispered, *"And you at the center, lost to the madness. A rogue Vampire whose only future was the True Death at the hands of the Directive."*

The words were spoken so matter-of-factly, so void of emotion that Alaric could only reply, *"Aye."*

He could feel Thaddeus waiting, his years of solitude affording him the ability to close his mind off to everything, sit in silence for as long as it took, and simply be. It was one of the many reasons Alaric thought so highly of his brother when Thad put his mind to something, nothing but God himself could change it.

Scratching at the stubble on his chin, Alaric continued, *"Since that time, my hunger has been insatiable. Bagged blood no longer sustains me. I need it fresh from the source. To feel their heartbeat quicken as my fangs penetrate their skin. To let their hot, coppery, life essence flow over my tongue, down my throat, satiating not only my hunger but the intense need burning through me as I fuck them over and over, taking them to the brink of death, holding them there for countless seconds then striking again, finishing the deed, only to seek out another, and another and..."*

"And you can find no relief?"

"No, none," he growled. *"And the Directive has sent their newest Enforcer to investigate a new rash of vampire related deaths. I must get this under control. They cannot know what is happening to me, or they will..."*

"Execute with extreme prejudice." Thaddeus finished Alaric's thought before going on. *"I am sorry, Brother. I have no knowledge of anything that comes close to what you are experiencing. Have you spoken to the Dragon? He is older than both of us and holds the wisdom of the ages passed down from his kin."* Pausing for a split-second the monk then added, *"He will also be able to help with the loss of control over your Dragon fire."*

"How did you...?"

"As it has always been, you lower your guard when you are speaking to me." There was a smile in Thaddeus' voice that Alaric hadn't heard in years. Maybe there still was hope for his solitary, guilt-ridden brother. However, saving Thaddeus would have to wait until Alaric could save himself.

"Thank you, Thaddeus. Not only for today, but for all the years you have been there. You are truly someone I can count on."

"Aye, and thank you, Alaric, my brother. Now, call the Dragon."

Once again the gates of Thad's mind slammed shut, leaving Alaric once again feeling as if the weight of the world was upon his shoulders. Opening the bright glowing link buried deep within his mind that he shared with Carrick, the Leader of the Golden Fire Clan of Dragons, Alaric called, *"Carrick?"*

"Alaric!" The Dragon's reply was quick and emphatic, filling the Vampire's mind with kinship and brotherly affec-

tion. *"How have you been? It has been nearly a decade since we've spoken."*

"Aye. I apologize for not keeping in touch life has been, well, I have no excuses. How have you been?"

"I am fine, but I can tell from the chaos in your mind that you are not."

That was Carrick, forever the Leader, always direct, always concerned, never backing down. Letting the pleasantries go, Alaric forged ahead. *"Aye, you are right, old friend. I fear I am slipping into the darkness of my kind. My hunger is insatiable, both for blood and for sex. I have had to stop taking blood from humans all together for fear that I will leave a trail of dead and drained bodies in my wake, but bagged blood does not to satisfy me. It is like filling the ocean with an eye dropper."* He paused, feeling the waves of comfort and healing Carrick was sending through the bond that they shared, touching the Dragon fire in the depths of Alaric's soul relieving its immediate need to rampage.

Before he could continue, Carrick spoke up, "Aye, I see your memories, of not only reality but of your dreams. I see the discourse and disruption, and it is something I have not seen in nearly a millennium. Even now, your hunger beats at me like an enemy's blade upon my shield. I can feel the fire in your veins, rising to meet the invisible invader that has stolen your control, taken your resolve."

"My gums ache as yours do. My skin feels as if it is being stretched beyond its reach, my muscles ache, my fangs long to retract, to tear and render nubile flesh, it is indeed maddening, but nothing you cannot handle."

Hanging on the Elder Dragon's every word, Alaric felt Carrick erect mental blocks to keep the madness from drawing him any farther into its abyss, before taking a deep breath and continuing, *"As I said, I have heard of this before.*

Our Ancients have even addressed it in the annals of Dragon history. But, to be sure, I must ask, is there anything that soothes your pain, relieves you of the hunger and need."

No sooner had the words been spoken than Ashlynn's beautiful face appeared, like a bright, shining light of all that was right and good in the world, at the forefront of Alaric's mind. *"Aye,"* he answered, an immediate and powerful wave of jealousy causing him to hide the doctor's glorious countenance from his old friend. *"I have."*

Laughter filled their bond as Carrick teased, *"You don't have to hide her from me. As I've told you many times over the years, the Universe has provided for her favored warriors by creating one perfect woman for each of us, the elusive piece of our soul, the one person in all the world who will complete us as no other."* Clearing his throat, the Dragon hurried on, *"And now, the time has come that I must tell you something I have been waiting to share since the moment we forged our bond. You, my brother, also have One that was made for you. One..."*

"What the hell are you talking about, Carrick? What bullshit are you shovelin'? I've come to you for help with my hunger, to help me reclaim my control, to harness the raging beast within, keep my head on my shoulders and not in a funeral pyre after being removed by an Enforcer's blade. What the fuck, man? Do you want me dead?"

"No." The Dragon's conviction and authority rang through Alaric's mind, followed closely by Carrick's irritation and impatience with the out of control vampire. *"What I want is for you to listen to what I'm saying, heed my words. It is you who came to me and now, you shall listen to what I have to say."* Going on, his voice returning to his usual cadence, the Elder Dragon explained, *"There is nearly an entire volume in the annals of Dragon History that tell of what your kin believe to be a myth, the Vampire's Thirst and the ever elusive bloodmate,*

the embodiment of your salvation, my friend. This woman is the light to your darkness, the fire to your ice, the only hope you have of bringing children into this world, of true love, of the mythical happily-ever-after we are all searching for no matter what we admit only to ourselves."

Unable to respond, shocked to his very core, Alaric thought back to the tales of the mystical bloodmate he'd heard from his grandmother even before the Christ child was born. Brygid would smile, her eyes would glaze over, and she would tell the stories she'd heard of the bloodmate. Alaric had always believed it to be a fairy tale, something contrived by the older ones to give those who came after them some hope of a 'normal' life.

Whatever the fuck normal is...

"*I heard that,*" Carrick snickered sarcastically. "*Being cheeky is not going to solve your problems, letting yourself believe and doing what is necessary is the only thing that will keep you from losing your mind and your life.*" The Dragon went on, "*What you are experiencing is the Vampire's Thirst, the all-too-real, visceral, gut-wrenching sign that your bloodmate is real, there and if you are to survive, you must claim her. Do I have your attention now?*"

"*Alright, I'm listening, but it's gonna take more than a few words from your history to convince me that my bloodmate has suddenly appeared after two thousand years. It's gonna take proof, hard evidence, not fairy tales.*"

"*Then let me ask you, as you're tearing through bags of blood and fucking your way through Dallas, have you found even a moment's peace?*"

Once again, Ashlynn's face appeared. Her deep brown eyes sparkled like finely polished onyx, her light brown hair, streaked with strands of pure sunlight grazed her porcelain cheeks just as his fingers ached to do. The scent of home, of poppies and buttercups, filled his senses, soothed his soul, gave his soul the peace he needed to see clearly.

"And there it is, all the proof I can give you. This woman, this Ashlynn, that not only your body but your heart and soul, long to bond with, is your Bloodmate. The one woman in all the world that can satiate your Thirst, give you back your control, and save your life."

Letting out the breath he was holding, Alaric remembered the pain, the agony he'd felt by letting Ashlynn dash away. In his crazed consciousness he'd known it was the right thing to do, that she was a doctor and someone might die without her help, but that hadn't stopped the craving, the searing ache in his gut, the twisting and cramping of every single muscle in his body, the fiery need to possess her – body, mind and soul - that forced him into the Chapel... the reason he'd called to his kin for help.

Be careful what you ask for because you just might get it...

10

Speeding into the Recovery Room, Ashlynn had a mere second of relief that the Code Blue was not for Timmy James before the healer in her took over and she raced over to help her colleague, Dr. Roberts, attempt to save his eighty-five-year-old patient, Mrs. Rabinowitz. Everyone on the team, doctors, nurses, techs, fought for nearly two hours to bring the jovial woman back to life, but it was not to be. Heaven gained another angel, one who had been a shining light to all who knew her for the better part of a century.

Walking beside Dr. Roberts, Ashlynn knew there were no words, that her friend only needed to know she was there if he needed her. Unlike what she would've done, Roberts didn't go to the Chapel, he instead went outside to the beautifully landscaped Courtyard and took a seat under the canopy of the limbs of the incredibly old oak tree.

Sitting on the same concrete bench, in the silence of the night, Ashlynn let her eyes slide shut as the cool night air blew the stray hairs off her cheeks and sounds of a quiet metropolis wrapped around her like a soft, fuzzy blanket.

She prayed for Mrs. Rabinowitz's family and the void that losing their matriarch would leave. She once again prayed for Timmy and the James family and for all the hospital staff who had committed themselves to save every life that they possibly could.

Her thoughts drifted as they always did when she'd had little to no sleep. Pictures of her childhood, images of her parents and grandparents, snapshots of laughter and good times with her friends, they all swirled together leading Ash to a place she didn't recognize. *Heather-covered the rolling hills. A soft, cool mist floated just above the lush green moors as the heavenly scent of fresh flowers, and rich earth filled her senses.*

Beautiful didn't begin to describe the vision. Although new, there was something familiar, inviting, welcoming about the place. The sound of horse hooves, something she was familiar with having grown up around all sorts of animals on her uncle's farm, Ash turned, her heart beating faster the closer the stranger galloped towards her.

Mesmerized by the rider's sharp features, his dark piercing eyes, and the way his long, dark hair flowed behind him like silken ribbons on the wind, Ashlynn could barely breathe. Smiling, unable to stop the joy at seeing him up close, she stood perfectly still as the man dressed in the blue and gray tartan of the MacAngoran Clan halted his stallion to her left and immediately jumped to the ground.

Closing the distance between them so quickly she hadn't seen him move, Ashlynn looked into the depths of his eyes, a perfect mix of cobalt blue and ashen charcoal as he wrapped his hands around hers. Shivers ran up her arms and down her spine at his touch. Looking to where their hands were intertwined, she imagined how perfectly his long, nimble fingers, like those of a pianist, would play her body like the most stunning concerto. Pulling her towards him, his strong arm around her waist making her tremble as the soft curves of her bosom met the muscular planes of his chest.

"Ashlynn." The whisper of her name of his lips was music to her ears. Lifting her eyes to his, she...

"Ashlynn. Ashlynn, wake up."

With her eyes flying open, she saw her own reflection in the lenses of Dr. Roberts' glasses as he went on with a chuckle, "I think you drifted off there, Ash."

Grinning along with her colleague, Ashlynn wiped the sleep from her eyes as she snickered, "I think you're right. It has definitely been a whopper of a couple of days."

"I know what you mean." Standing up to his full height, Roberts' added, "You need a lift home?"

"No, I think I'll go check on my patient in Recovery and then grab a nap in my office." She got up and followed the other doctor back inside.

"Okay, if you're sure. It's no trouble. I go right past your place."

Waving him off, knowing he was not only trying to be nice but also was sure to ask her out for about the hundredth time, Ash smiled, "Thanks anyway, Jason. I really need to check on Timmy, and I have rounds this evening."

Looking more than a little putout but still smiling, Roberts' nodded, "Take Care. See you later."

Watching him walk away, Ashlynn felt bad that she didn't share Jason Roberts' feeling. Sure, he was a nice guy and not at all bad looking – there just simply were no sparks. Nothing. Nada. Zilch. He did absolutely nothing for her, and in her mind, that just wouldn't do.

"Life is too short," she murmured to herself, walking down the hall towards the elevator. Pressing the arrow that pointed downward, she thought about her dream, or rather, the man in her dream. She'd seen him before. Recognized the gorgeous jawline, the high cheekbones, the devilish glint in his eye.

Still lost in thought, she stepped into the elevator, pushed the button to the basement and walked to the back of the car. Leaning her hip on the metal railing, her dream from the past morphed into a memory from several hours earlier.

She saw the man outside the Chapel, the one she'd nearly bowled over. The icy hot chill of his touch, the same that she'd experienced in her dream, the one she felt when...

"Oh crap, where was it? I know I've... That's it!" She cheered, spinning on her toes as the elevator door opened and there, not ten feet from her stood the very man from her dream, the one that had saved her from falling, the one she looked at nearly every night on the cover of a magazine.

Throwing her arm out in front of her chest, pointing directly at his heart, she declared, "It's you!"

11

"You've been haunting my dreams," Ashlynn blurted out, before slapping her hand over her mouth and blushing the most alluring shade of red Alaric had ever witnessed.

Striding into the elevator, unable to stop, needing to be near her more than he needed his next breath, Alaric closed the doors with the nod of his head, laid the palms of his hands against the cool, stainless-steel panel, he caged her in, staring deep into the warmth of her dazzling brown eyes.

Leaning his body towards her, only a single breath of air separating him from her, he whispered, "And what have you seen?"

Watching so intently he forgot to breathe as just the tip of her tongue wet her bottom lip, he heard her heart fluttering like the wings of a hummingbird and the rush of her blood through her veins as the elevator filled with the warm, succulent scent of poppies and buttercups. She wanted him as much as he wanted her. The time had come, he had found his haven from the Thirst, and it was Ashlynn. She would be his.

Laying his lips to hers, trying to go slow, praying he wasn't scaring her, but needing her with every fiber of his being, Alaric gently nibbled and teased her tender flesh until he was sure he would go mad. Sliding his hands down the wall, his arms wrapping around her waist, he pulled her closer, groaning deep in his throat when her hands cupped his face, and she opened to him.

Deepening their kiss, feeling the chaotic miasma that his soul and mind had become unraveling, setting itself to rights, he could no longer hold back. His hands roamed her body, his fingers finding the soft, round globes of her ass, he lifted her feet from the floor, pushing her back against the wall as she wrapped her legs around his waist.

Dominating her mouth, seeking ownership of her heart and soul, Alaric rolled his hips to hers, pushing his erection against the heat of her center. Moans of her sweet surrender filled their embrace as Ashlynn pushed her hips against his. He could feel her desire growing, blooming, exploding into a roaring fire, encompassing them both.

Her hands dove into his hair. The short flat tips of her nails dug into his scalp. The need to taste her, to drink from her vein overwhelmed him. Tearing his lips from hers, Alaric kissed across her jaw, teased her ear with his tongue and teeth, whispering sweet nothings as he made his way to the decadent temptation of her neck.

Lavishing her pounding pulse, his canines extending, he touched her mind, using the magic of his Druid heritage combined with that of the Dragons which he'd been given by his bond with Carrick he murmured, *"May I taste you, my sweet? May I take your essence into my soul? Will you calm the beast that lives within me?"*

"Yes, oh yes." Her answer came almost immediately,

adamantly and without fear, as she let her head fall to the side, granting him access to her vein.

Sliding the tips of his fangs over her jugular, inhaling her delectable scent, his heart sped, beating in time with hers as he slowly, lovingly pierced her porcelain skin. As the first drop of Ashlynn's life essence flowed over his lips onto his tongue, all his senses intensified. Lights flashed like fireworks in the sky behind his closed eyelids. The fiery heat of Ashlynn's skin burned through the rough cotton of her scrubs, scorching his fingers. His cock thrust against the deep ridges of his zipper pushing to be buried deep within its mate.

Thrusting forward, her hips moving in sync with every sip he took from her neck, Ashlynn moaned his name, her voice echoing off the cold, steel of the elevator walls as her hands slid from his hair onto his shoulders, her nails scratching the leather of his jacket. Fearing he would take too much, Alaric withdrew his fangs, licking the tiny marks left by his fangs to stop the flow of blood.

Smiling against her skin as her hand returned to his head in an attempt to push his lips back to her throat, Ashlynn begged with her mewling whimpers for him to continue. Holding tight to her bum with one hand as his other slipped under her top, around the waist of her pants and into the front of her silk panties, he teased the wet curls covering her pussy. Pushing his hips tighter still against Ashlynn's as she thrust upward, trying to force his fingers where she needed them most, Alaric leaned his head back, gazing at the most beautiful sight he'd ever seen.

Slipping first one then another finger inside her pussy, his fangs ached with the need to once again be buried in her vein as Ashlynn wailed, "Yes...yes, oh, please Alaric, yes."

Moving his digits in and out, over and over, driving her

passion higher and higher, he pressed his thumb against her throbbing clit as he commanded, "Look at me, Ashlynn. Acknowledge the man whose heart and soul you own."

Spearing him with a look of utter desire, riding his fingers to her climax, Ashlynn growled, "Yes, Alaric, yes."

In that split-second of time, less than a heartbeat, the ancient vampire's world was turned upside-down and inside-out. Her desire became his. He was lost to everything that they were together, in a world where only they existed, one he never wanted to leave.

Feeling her orgasm very near its peak, Alaric slid a third finger inside Ashlynn, bent the tips in a come-hither motion that teased the sensitive bundle of nerves deep within her that he knew would drive her to completion, and watched in awe as her eyes were forced shut, and she threw back her head in utter bliss. Ashlynn's mouth opened wide in a silent scream, her pussy closed tight around his digits, sucking them in as far as they could go as over and over she came, her climax rocking her body to its very core.

Slowing his motions as her juices wet his fingers, flowing over his hand and wrist, Alaric laid butterfly kisses on her eyelids, cheeks, and chin as his Ashlynn floated back to earth. Waiting for her eyes to once again open, Alaric felt her body go limp. Letting go of her bottom and letting her feet slide to the floor, the ancient vampire's heart nearly ceased to beat as he realized Ashlynn was unconscious.

Looking into her mind, listening intently to the beat of her heart and the sounds of her still ragged breathing, Alaric breathed a sigh of relief to find that she had only fainted. Smiling slyly, proud that he'd been able to give his Bloodmate such bliss, he lifted, Ashlynn into his arms and kissed her forehead, reveling in the electricity of their connection as it skittered across his already sparking nerve-endings. Exiting the elevator, not wanting to be seen with one of their most-valued doctors unconscious in his arms, the ancient vampire raced from the hospital using his preternatural speed, slowing only when he was hidden in the shadows of the alley leading to *CRAVE* and his home.

Climbing the iron fire escape he'd had installed for just such an occasion, Alaric climbed onto the balcony, opened the sliding glass doors with his mind and walked straight into his bedroom where he gently laid Ashlynn in the middle of his bed. Pulling a chair closer, he shed his jacket, took off his boots and sat down, needing to be near her, watch her, memorize her stunning features as she slept.

Leaning forward, Alaric reached for her hand as he laid his head on the cool, soft cotton of his stark white duvet. Letting his eyes close, more content than he could ever remember being, the ancient vampire sighed, "Finally, the sweet release of peace, the beauty of the woman who owns my heart and a future unfolding with its many wonders before us. I can only hope she wakes with the same sentiment upon her lovely lips."

12

Not wanting to wake from the best dream she'd ever had, Ashlynn squeezed her eyes shut and rolled to her other side, ignoring the enticing scent of coffee and cinnamon rolls as she pulled the incredibly soft blanket over her head. Floating in and out of slumber, she smiled as *his* voice, the rumbling, rolling lilt that had seduced not only her body, but her mind and soul, filled the room as if he were not only a figment of her incredibly active imagination, but a real living, breathing man whom with she could live out every one of her naughty little fantasies.

Flashes of his face, his eyes, his gorgeously muscled body flashed in her mind, warming her body, making her long to have his lips, his hands, his fangs on her body once again.

Whoa! Fangs? Leslie was right, I do need to get out more. But, maybe...

Pondering making love to a vampire, wondering what it would feel like to actually have him drinking from her, Ash rolled onto her back, pushed her long curls off her face and slowly opened her eyes. Gazing at the stark white ceiling above her, she shoved the duvet down to her waist and finished her uncovering ritual by kicking with her feet until the blanket was in a pile at the foot of the bed.

Turning her head to the left to see what time it was, the reality of her situation came racing at her like a runaway train. That was not her nightstand or her clock. She was not in her bed...or her room...or her own clothes.

Jumping out of the bed, looking for an exit, she once again heard the very male, very sexy voice making her whisper, "Son of a bitch, he's real." Taking two steps towards the bathroom, deciding she would see if any of the hundreds of stupid movies she'd watched on lifetime were right and she could escape through the window in there, Ashlynn stopped dead in her tracks.

Slapping her hand to her neck, she felt two wounds, no larger than the head of a pin right over her jugular. Racing to the bathroom, needing to find a mirror and fast, she spun to her right, leaned as far over the vanity as she could and stared at the tiny, red marks.

"It was real?" The words slipped out as she forced herself to breathe. "I had sex in an elevator with a virtual stranger?" Looking at her reflection, wondering if her eyes could get any bigger or her mouth could open any wider, Ashlynn nearly jumped out of her skin, complete with a shriek and her hand slapping over her chest, when Alaric simply appeared out of thin air and propped his hip against the doorframe.

"Good morning, sweet Ashlynn. How did you sleep?"

Gawking at literally the sexiest man alive, at least in her opinion, Ash worked hard not to faint or throw up or both. Her mind was racing, searching for what had truly happened and what was a dream when her eyes landed on the perfectly sculpted muscles of Alaric's chest and torso.

Her fingers tingled as her body warmed, and her mind screamed, *"It was all real, you idiot!"*

Still mute and apparently losing whatever of her mind that was left, her gaze continued its perusal of his physique while she tried to come up with a logical explanation for her undeniable need to rush into his arms and bare not only her neck but her body to the man, check...make that *Vampire*, before her.

"It is quite simple, you see," his Scottish brogue was music to her ears and only added to her desire to strip off his jeans and see what other pleasures laid beneath the distressed denim. "And something that until not even a day ago, I thought was only a myth...a fairy tale told to those of us made Vampire."

As his words sunk into her confused, lust-addled, freaking-out brain, Ashlynn's mouth opened before said brain engaged and she shrieked, "You kissed me in an elevator!"

"Aye, I did," he winked, the corner of his full pink lips curling up in a sexy smirk. "And so much more."

He stepped forward.

She stepped backward.

He turned his head to the side, his eyes narrow as if he was about to ask a question.

She beat him to the punch, still thinking before she thought. "You drank my blood. You kissed me."

"You said that already, my sweet," Alaric interjected.

"You...you...your... f-f-fin..." Ash ignored what he said, rushing on, pointed at his hands, vividly remembering how those nimble fingers had made her body sing and trying to hide both her excitement and desire.

Lifting his hand and wiggling his fingers, Alaric once again interrupted. "My fingers? Oh yes, they did..."

"Stop right there." Ashlynn pointed at him, grabbing hold of her embarrassment and turning it into outrage. She took a step forward. "What is this?" She motioned back-and-forth between them. "Why did you do that? Why? Did you accost me in the elevator?" She took another step forward, trying to be intimidating, but actually being drawn to the damn man like a moth to a flame.

Yeah, and those stupid suckers get zapped and die...

"Why did it feel so right? Why didn't I fight you off? Why in all that is holy did I let you bite me?" She took the final step forward, staring right into his eyes. Her heart was racing. She was short of breath. Tiny beads of sweat were sliding down her spine. Her words were coming so fast she sounded like an auctioneer. As she poked Alaric right in his bare chest to punctuate every word. "Who are you, really? Did you screw with my mind? I've heard Vampires can do that, but I never believed it. Did you put a spell on me? Are spells even real? What am I doing here? Where are my clothes? Am I your servant or your blood slave or whatever the hell you call them?" Snapping the fingers on her free hand as she poked him even harder in the chest, Ashlynn exclaimed, "Renfield! That's it. That's the name. Am I gonna be your Renfield?'

Slapping the palm of her hand over his heart, she gasped at the icy hot sparks that danced up her arms as goose bumps rose all over her body. "Will you talk? Will you answer at least one of my questions? What the hell is wrong with you? Do you make it a habit of kissing women, making their fantasies come true and then locking them away in your...your... yo...

Ashlynn's words instantly evaporated as Alaric slammed

his lips to her. Pulling her to him, his arms wrapped around her waist, the blazing heat of his body threatening her very fantasy, Ashlynn was helpless but to do as he bid. Opening completely, she moaned low in her throat as his hands roamed her body, leaving a fiery trail in their wake.

Arousal thickened in her blood, growing by leaps and bounds with each swipe of his tongue alongside hers. She whimpered at his bold moves as he delved farther into her, their bodies, hearts, and souls in perfect union. Fanning the flames of her desire with his drugging moves, it was as if he read her mind, knowing what she wanted...what she needed, even before she did.

Her panties were soaked as he rocked his hips between her legs, the hard length of his erection teasing her clit making it throb with the need to come. Raking her nails down his back, Ashlynn pulled him closer, holding onto his shoulders as he gripped her ass and lifted her off the floor.

Wrapping her legs around his waist, pulling him closer still as his lips left hers and kissed along her jaw, Ashlynn leaned her head to the side as she whispered, "It is yours for the taking."

Throwing back his head, Alaric roared, the declaration of raw passion and absolute possession making the need for Ashlynn to feel him buried nearly unbearable. She wanted all of him, his cock, his fangs, his heart and his soul. Gone were the questions, the doubts, the uncertainty, nothing had ever felt so right, so wonderful.

Turning quickly and making it to the bed before Ash had barely realized they'd moved, she grumbled her discontent and tried to pull Alaric down with her as he gently laid her on the bed. Grinning with mischief, he gave her a sexy growl, "Put your hands over your head and stay right where you are."

Trembling with excitement, she followed his orders, watching closely as he dropped to his knees, and slowly began kissing across her ankle and up the inside of her leg. Gripping the duvet tighter the closer to her center he climbed, Ash tried with all her might to lay still and not close her legs as her arousal soared, the proof wetting the inside of her thighs.

Licking the wetness from her legs, Alaric groaned low in his throat, whispering, "Aye, ye taste like heav'n."

Throwing back her head, wailing his name, her eyes rolling back in her head as he teased her throbbing clit through the damp silk of her panties, Ashlynn's back bowed off the bed, when he fingers slipped inside, through her wet curls, thrusting deeply into her pussy. Lifting her hips, willing him farther inside, her orgasm speeding to its triumphant completion, her mind and body blew apart as Alaric touched her g-spot with the tips of his fingers, squeezed her clit under his thumb and sank his fangs into the pulsing vein at the very top inside her thigh.

Over and over she came, her orgasms in perfect time with every long, thorough draw he took of her blood. Gasping for air, never wanting to leave the perfect moment in time Alaric had created for her, Ashlynn's body shuddered as he pulled his fangs from her flesh and licked the insignificant marks she knew were there.

Climbing onto the bed, with the grace and swagger of a jungle cat and gloriously naked, the tip of his cock sliding across the soaking crotch of her panties, Ashlynn's hips rose to meet his as Alaric chuckled, "In due time, my sweet. Somethin' this perfect must be savored."

No sooner had he spoken the words than he reached between them, rip the flimsy silk from her body and threw it over his shoulder. "But then again, savoring is overrated."

"Oh yes, it is." Shouting her last word as the tip of Alaric's erection pushed through her curls and into her throbbing pussy, Ashlynn's hands flew to his shoulders as her legs wrapped around his hips, her ankles crossed and she forced him into her body as far as he could go.

Holding perfectly still, staring into the eyes of the man she was already falling in love with, she refused to think, forcing herself to only feel as her body adjusted to his size. Ever so slightly rolling her hips, teasing Alaric as he'd teased her, Ashlynn knew the exact second she'd pushed her Vampire too far as his ash-blue eyes turned a deep gunmetal gray and the tips of his fangs bit into his bottom lip.

Pulling out of her so far that she tightened her legs around his waist to keep him from completely retreating, Alaric smiled a devilish smile as he plunged back into her, immediately pulling out then repeating the action, creating a perfect rhythm Ash fought to match. Awash with so many sensations, so many emotions, so very much of absolutely everything, everything Ashlynn felt as if she was being reborn, seeing the world for the first time through the eyes of the man who was capturing her heart with his every move.

Feeling another earth-shattering orgasm thundering through her body, she thrust her fingers into his long dark hair, fisted the silken tresses and dragged his lips to her neck. "Bite me, Alaric. Love me. I am yours."

Goosebumps rose on her flesh as he taunted the overly sensitive skin of her neck with his fangs. She heard his whispered promise of, "As I am yours," just as the sharp points of his canines pierced her vein.

Wringing climax after climax from her until Ash ran the blunt tips of her nails down his back, her pussy gripping his throbbing cock as her hips pounded against his and her heels dug into the hard muscles of his ass. The pull of his fangs from her flesh made her pussy grip his cock with a renewed vigor pushing Alaric over the edge as he threw back his head, diving deeper still into her. Roaring her name so loudly she was sure the windows rattled, Alaric emptied himself into her over and over bringing yet another orgasm from her.

Letting his head drop forward, Alaric captured Ashlynn's eyes with a powerful look of possession and passion as he took her lips in a slow, sensual kiss that touched not only her heart but her very soul. Sliding his arms under her, he slipped his cock from her as he rolled them over on their sides, facing one another with their heads on the pillows at the head of the bed.

Looking into one another eyes, Ashlynn was just about to ask about the magnificent dragon tattoo whose head was over Alaric's heart while the rest of his body covered the left side of the Vampire's body when he lifted his head, sniffed the air and bellowed, "Fire!"

13

As the acrid scent of burning petrol and the unmistakable heat of an open fire filled his penthouse, Alaric pulled Ashlynn into his arms, jumped out of bed, and set her by his closet as he grabbed clothes for both of them. Shoving a pair of sweats and jacket in her hands, he ordered, "Put these on," while shoving his legs into a pair of jeans and his feet into his boots.

Grabbing her shoes, he wrapped his arms around her waist and headed out onto the terrace, going down the same fire escape he gone up the night before. Calling to Ruari, glad his friend lived next door above *The Galley*, Alaric ordered, *"Call the fire department. CRAVE is on fire."*

Stepping onto the concrete of the alley behind the club, he dropped Ashlynn's shoes and set her feet next to them as he called to Sampson, *"Come now. There's a fire at the club. Bring Axel."*

Not waiting for an answer, he quickly scrolled through his contacts, hit the one marked MATEO and before the newest Enforcer could even say hello, snarled, "My club's on fire. Come do your job." Disconnecting the call as the other

Vampire was speaking, Alaric handed the phone to Ashlynn and pointed to the covered porch on the backside of *The Galley.*

Hearing the sirens at the precise moment Ruari appeared, he wrapped his fingers around Ashlynn's upper arms, looked her right in the eye and for the only time in his life he could ever remember, the ancient Vampire begged, "Please don't follow me into the club. I can hear your thoughts. I know that you plan to be right by my side, but I cannot do what I must if I am worried about your safety." Motioning with his head, he added, "Go over there. Stay out of harm's way. I will come for you."

He could feel her resistance, her need to help and immediately appealed to the Healer within her. "In the closet in *The Galley*, there's a large first aid kit. Go get that and help any who are injured. Your handprint is already programmed into the ID pad at all the entrances."

Smiling as his astounding Bloodmate turned and rushed away, Alaric followed Ruari through the backdoor of *CRAVE*, into the supply closet and grabbed a huge fire extinguisher. Each walking through one of the sets of double doors that led from the kitchen into Silk Fantasies, the ancient Vampire stopped cold as a familiar scent, one he hadn't encountered since leaving the bonny shores of Scotland in 1716 rose over the dark, billowing smoke.

"Can you smell that?" He asked Ruari, careful to keep his mental blocks locked tight as he sprayed white foam from the hose attached to the fire extinguisher in his other hand.

"You mean the rancid smell of Scotch malt, Buckfast, and a fuckin' useless, traitor of a Vampire?" Ruari yelled above the roar of the fire, quickly answering his own question, "Yeah, I smell the son of a whore, but I can't see him, and the scent of human blood is much stronger."

Putting the flames wherever he could, Alaric crossed the huge dancefloor making his way to the bar where he could see the outline of his Second through the haze of smoke and falling ash. Looking behind the scorched wood and soot-covered granite he could barely believe his eyes. There, decorated with thousands of scorched, bloody white rose petals was a sickening pile of drained human torsos and severed arms and legs.

Moving closer, shocked at the extra attention the killer had shown by creating a perimeter of wet bar towels around the bloody body parts, making sure they were not engulfed in flames before they could be found. Pounding footsteps and orders hollered through a megaphone drew Alaric's attention as the firemen came through the front and back of the club dousing the fire with gallon upon gallon of water.

Working alongside the first responders for countless hours, Alaric, Ruari, and Sampson helped to extinguish the blaze until Mateo finally arrived, asking them to meet him outside. Walking through the ruins of his club, the smoldering remains of one of his most profitable businesses, Alaric led the way out the back, thanking his employees who had shown up with water, Gatorade and food for all the firemen and EMTs who fought to save their place of employment.

Shielding his eyes from the late afternoon sun, Alaric looked all around for Ashlynn, calling to her as he walked towards Mateo and the others. Not worried when she didn't answer, assuming she was at the First Aid station the EMTs has set up at the back of *The Galley* he stopped next Ruari and asked, "What do you need? As you can see, we're a bit busy here."

"Yes, and I'm very sorry for the loss of your club and for those who were indiscriminately hacked to bits by the rogue. We have determined this is the work of one Vampire and you are his target."

Mateo was scrolling through his phone not making eye contact until Alaric snarled, "You fucking think so, Mat?" He purposely used the Enforcer's nickname just to piss him off. "You think I'm the target?" He glared at the Enforcer as he pointed at what was left of *CRAVE*. "Let's see, he's done everything but write down the address to every murder. He's used my family's crest, my grandmother's ring, the tartan of my Clan and written a note in Gaelic with one of his victim's blood." Taking an aggressive step forward, furious that the Directive had let it get as far as they had, he roared, "Now, why the fuck are you wasting my time instead of catching the crazy motherfucker."

"So, you know who it is?"

Mateo looked shocked, making Alaric think about ripping the Enforcer's head from his shoulders and throwing it into the few flames still burning at the corner of his club. Poking Mateo in the chest, he ground out, "It's got to be Androu. It can be no other. I told you I couldn't locate him, that he wasn't responding, and that he was the only other who would have had access to Brygid's ring. What the fuck are you waiting for?"

Unfortunately, Alaric never got to hear Mateo's response as one of the younger firemen came running out of the club, holding a small metal box and calling to him. Turning towards the man in silver fire gear with a respirator hanging around his neck, the ancient Vampire waved his hand, stepping away from Mateo and holding out his hand.

"We found this beside the bodies," the fireman stated, handing Alaric the box. "It's so scorched there won't be any fingerprints, so the Captain said I could bring it to you. I made sure it was cool enough to handle."

"Thank you so much," Alaric forced a smile. "Please be sure to get something to eat and drink and tell all your mates."

"Thank you, Sir."

Turning back towards Ruari and Sampson, ignoring Mateo, Alaric opened the box, lifted out a stack of pictures that were laid face down with a large scrolling script inked on the back. Reading the words, his blood ran cold, and his rage caught fire. "*A Bloodmate for the traitor. This simply cannot stand. Bring me what you took all those years ago and you may retrieve the body of your beloved where the bodies of the freed African-Americans were laid to rest.*"

Dropping the box and racing to *The Galley*, Alaric immediately saw that Ashlynn was frighteningly absent from the scene. Slamming his hand against the ID pad, he nearly ripped the heavy mirrored-glass door from its hinges as he raced to find his Bloodmate as dread filled his soul.

Stopping dead in his tracks as the scent of Ashlynn's blood smacked him square in the face, he gaped at what used to be a stark white wall leading to the vault and read the words painted in his Bloodmate's blood aloud, "*A thabhairt duit, Deartháir.*"

Walking straight to the farthest corner of the building, he stepped into the private elevator, pushed the button marked U and as he descended to the underground garage only very few knew existed, the enraged ancient vampire whispered, "Aye, to me it is, Brother, and may God have mercy on your soulless hide when I find you."

14

———

She'd heard the sound of one of the doors of *The Galley* opening and closing, had been sure it was Sampson since Alaric had called the Viking before sending her away and hollered over her shoulder for him to come help her find the First Aid kit in the enormous closet. No sooner had the words left her mouth than the creepy feeling of spiders crawling up her spine made her shiver and the stench of old beer and stale whiskey nearly made her gag.

Slowly standing up, she turned towards the smell and tried not to react as she took in the eerie, gaunt man standing behind her. Tall, lanky to the point of being nearly emaciated, with his long black hair matted in clumps as it hung in oily strings well past his shoulder, the stranger's nearly transparent skin confirmed that he was a Vampire even before she saw his fangs as he smirked in her direction.

Trying to muster the courage to speak, Ashlynn refused to be bullied as she threw back her shoulders in defiance when the Vampire lisped around his fangs, sounding more like a snake than a man, "Sso, thiss iss what all the fusss iss about? The bastard'ss Bloodmate."

"If you're looking for Alaric, he's over at *CRAVE* fighting the fire." She pointed, proud that she'd kept the tremble from her voice and attempting to distract the Vampire long enough to figure out how to contact Alaric with that mind trick he kept using. "Do you know where that is?"

Yeah, it was a stupid question, but she was still trying to call to Alaric. Stepping forward, the unnerving Vamp slowly shook his head, "Nay, I have found who I want."

Moving back as the man raised his fist, Ash didn't even get the chance to scream as the jerk opened his hand and blew some kind of nasty smelling shit right into her face. Coughing and sputtering, she remembered falling backward before her world went completely black. The whole fainting and waking up in weird places was getting really old, especially since this time there was no sexy Alaric.

Musty, decayed, and bitter, the scent of old bones, long-forgotten earth and formaldehyde filled her nose making her eyes water as her hacking cough echoed through the darkness. Just as if someone or worse yet, *something*, had heard her thoughts, a torch, hanging from a sconce on the far side of the room burst to life. Once her eyes had adjusted to the sudden influx of light, Ash immediately wished she was back in the dark and unconscious.

Looking up and down one wall and then the other, she counted over eighty crypts in what she now knew was a mausoleum. Squinting to read their names, she saw things like Jezebel, Matthias, Adam, Ezekiel. Pushing her sight as hard as she could, she was finally able to make out what at first had seemed like a strange emblem but soon she recognized as pictures of broken shackles.

"The Old Dallas Burial Ground," she murmured, trying

to show reverence and her respect to the cemetery that was formed in the early 1840s in an impromptu manner when the first death to occur in the newly formed village of Dallas dictated its necessity.

She remembered visiting the graveyard in her undergraduate years while taking forensic biology. Professor McKinnley's voice still rang in her ears, his deep Texas drawl somehow adding to the importance of the place. *"Now, students, it is important to think of all factors when searching for forensic evidence, not just what you find on that remains of the deceased. You must look at the whole picture, for example, this mausoleum, as well as the cemetery as a whole, is highly atypical for the antebellum South. The Old Dallas Burial Ground which was later named Freedman's Cemetery marks the final resting place of white settlers, enslaved African Americans, and freed slaves."*

"Researchers have found that Freedman's Cemetery's origin ultimately traces back to a slave cemetery that later became the first ever communal graveyard and led to the name of the town of Freedman, in which men of all races were considered free and could own land."

"Kind of ironic that you find yourself shackled to the statue of St. Benedict the Black, the patron saint of freed slaves." He walked around her, talking in a haughty tone with one arm behind his back like a nobleman and the other motioning as if he was addressing Parliament. The only comfort that she could find was that he was no longer lisping which meant his sharp, deadly fangs were no longer showing and he was talking instead of draining her dry. All she could do was pray Alaric would find her before Cuckoo Pants ripped her to shreds.

"Did you know that the Italian black Catholic saint's, Benedict, was the son of African slaves. He gained sainthood because he inspired black identity and pride. I wonder if there will ever be a Vampire saint. Don't you think there should be? We are, after all, the superior race."

Not answering the raving lunatic, Ashlynn tried to untie the ropes securing her hands behind her back. She may not be able to outrun the fucker, and fighting him was a fool's errand, but she damned sure wasn't prepared to die with her ass in the dirt while some deranged asshole gave her a history lesson.

Stopping in front of her and smiling, the asshole Vampire surmised, "I'm sure you have questions." Standing so close to Ashlynn's outstretched feet that she jerked them towards her body as she craned her neck to look up at his grossly decorated face, the idiot actually smiled – one that reached all the way to his beady black, soulless eyes making them sparkle in the firelight. It was literally the creepiest thing she'd ever seen, and she oversaw the insect breeding program at Harvard for a year-and-a-half.

Taking in the layers of dried, caked-on blood, dirt, bits of hair and flesh, she shoved the bile rising in her throat back, tried to school her expression and nodded, "Yes. Why am I here?"

"Excellent question, my dear. You really are as smart as they all say."

Wondering who '*they*' were, but was working so hard not to throw up that she had to breathe through her mouth while sitting perfectly still as the crazed predator before her went back to walking and talking.

"You are here simply because you, lovely girl, are the only thing in this world that Alaric loves. You," once again he stopped right in front of her, "Are the only thing I can take from him that will make him understand the pain I have suffered for nearly four hundred years."

Remembering something she'd learned in an Abnormal Psychology class about speaking to someone who was suffering a psychotic break, Ashlynn took a deep breath, slowly letting it out, kept her tone soft and even and coaxed, "I am so very sorry for your loss. Would you like to tell me what happened?" Then recalling that she was supposed to use his name as much as possible, she smiled and asked, "Can I know your name?"

Praying with all her might that she could keep Captain Crazy talking, she continued to look into the void that was his gaze as the Vampire responded, "I am Androu, of Clan MacAngoran and your Beloved's Maker."

Holding her smile while stuffing her shock at the fact that the Vampire before her could have had anything to do with the man she'd spent the last twenty or so hours with, Ash sweetly replied, "It is nice to meet you, Androu."

Barely nodding to acknowledge her words, the Psycho went on, "Alaric betrayed us, every member of our Clan, every person who ever loved and cared for him, by leaving Scotland and heading to the New World. He left us when we needed him most, when the Jacobites were invading our island." Kneeling down to her right, so close that she could feel his cold, fetid breath on her cheek, he seethed, "He left his dear grandmother, Brygid, the woman I loved more than my eternal life, the only woman who ever truly saw me for what I was, and appreciated me, to die, to lose her head on the battlefield like so much fodder for the Duke of Agryll's war."

Leaning even closer, his spittle bathing her face, the lunatic spat, "That bastard Sir John Campbell thought it was funny to mount my dear Brygid's head on a pike outside MacAngoran Castle with a placard reading *The Queen is No More.*" Grabbing her face with such force that the ragged tips of his nails dug into her skin, Androu jerked her head towards his until they were eye-to-eye and with a maniacal cackle added, "But you see, Brygid and I were meant to be together forever, to live out eternity side-by-side." He gripped her hair even tighter. "So, in the dead of night when the fool was sleeping, I saved my dear Brygid. I took her back."

Flinging Ash's head backward with such force that her skull bounced off the statue behind her, the crazed Vampire dashed across the room, returning as quickly as he left with a duffle bag he waved in front of her face like some sort of flag. Trying to clear her vision, her head pounding like a bass drum in a marching band from Androu's abuse, Ashlynn gagged as he hand disappeared into the bag only to instantaneously reappear with the decomposed skull of what she could only assume was Brygid.

Holding the bones of the woman he obviously loved with a tenderness that belied everything Ashlynn knew of the deranged psychopath, Androu smoothed the dark, dry strands of hair remaining on the skull as he added, "I can only hope Alaric will also keep what remains of you after I have disposed of you. It is, after all, what one owes his one true Bloodmate."

15

Speeding down every back street and alley to avoid detection and get to the other side of town as quickly as possible, Alaric tuned out everything and everyone, including Ruari and Sampson as he raced to save Ashlynn. Slowing to a crawl, he let his Harley idle as he rolled up next to the tall iron arch announcing one of the entrances to the sacred land.

Watching the last rays of the sun disappear over the horizon, he parked his motorcycle and followed the scent of buttercups and poppies to the very back of the cemetery. Standing outside the only mausoleum in the entire acre graveyard, Alaric tried to reach Ashlynn telepathically only to find that Androu had blanketed the structure in a thick blanket of Druid mysticism.

Not surprised to find the stone and iron door unlocked, he slowly entered the crypt, the scent of Ashlynn's blood making his fangs extend and the beast within roar with the need to save the one meant to be theirs. Walking through the first alcove, down a dank, dark corridor, he saw the flickering light of a torch mere seconds before he saw the face of his Bloodmate.

Forcing himself to stay put, looking at the rivulets of blood flowing down her face from the small half-moon slices in her cheek, obviously caused by Androu's nails, Alaric stifled the growl festering in his chest. He would rip the bloody bastard to shreds, burn his body until there was nothing left but a pile of ashes and then spread the soot to the four corners of the earth. Androu would be no more, not even a footnote in the annals of time, a nuisance well disposed of like the vermin he was.

Sensing the rogue's presence but unable to locate him, Alaric kept his eyes trained on Ashlynn as he pushed the pure magic of the Dragons through the structure finally able to hear the slow, sluggish heartbeat of his Maker.

Clap! Clap! Clap!

The mockingly slow clap of hands echoed through the mausoleum closely followed by a voice Alaric had spent four centuries trying to forget. "Look at this, Ashlynn. He came. The mighty Alaric MacLauren, son of the Chieftain *Monadh Croibhe*, grandson of Brygid, Leader of Clan MacAngoran, a royal from the olde country, come to save the day."

The tall, shadowy figure moved through the shadows, protected by strong Druid magic that pricked at Alaric's flesh as he continued, "Where is your lapdog? Where are your followers." Cackling like the madman he was, Androu added, "Do not tell me you've come alone? Has the coward actually decided to fight a fair fight, man-to-man for the first time in his life?"

"What are you blathering on about, Androu? Was it not you who hung on Brygid's every word? Suffered her every folly? Licked up whatever table scraps she left?" Alaric taunted as the heat of the rogue Vampire's mysticism grew. Keeping his eyes trained on Ashlynn, Alaric tried again to reach her, wondering why she sat so still, so silent, not moving in the slightest.

"Isn't that my grandmother's magic I feel you wielding," he snarled. "How does it feel to have stolen all Brygid secrets, sold her out to enemies and then left her to die while you cowered in the shadows?" Stepping into the light, trying to draw Androu out while getting closer to his Bloodmate, Alaric jeered, "Tell, me, *Maker*," the word was fiery with venom, "Do your followers know what an utter bastard you are?" Scratching at the stubble on his chin, over exaggerating his contemplation as he took another tenuous step towards Ashlynn, he added, "Or have they abandoned you? Seen you for what you really are? Left you to drown in your own madness? Are you alone, Androu? Have you sought me out so that you may drag me into the pits of your own personal hell?"

An unholy roar ricocheted off the stone walls as if out of thin air Androu materialized, flying through the air, sword arced over his head, eyes trained on Alaric's neck. Launching himself towards Ashlynn, the ancient Vampire landed only inches in front of his Bloodmate, ducking just in time to miss the reckless swing of his Maker's blade.

Rolling away to the side, Alaric felt the sparks of Dragon fire dancing on his fingertips but feared catching Ashlynn in the crossfire. Looking for anything he could use as a weapon, Androu once again began to rant. "I did what I had to do to survive."

Slashing his blade in Alaric's direction, he wailed, "It is *you* who broke her heart. *You* who left your last living kin in search of a new life, wealth and fame in the New World. My Brygid..." Androu bared his fangs and hissed. "My beautiful love, the woman who owned my heart and soul... It was YOU!" With every word, his voice became more hysterical. "She never got over your desertion. Every day she plotted and planned behind my back. Went to those who were loyal to her, who believed her lies. Made them promise to keep her treacherous secrets."

Madness burned in the depths of his soulless eyes, Androu was well and truly gone, not only was he rogue, but he was also deranged and psychotic. Over and over he slashed his blade, driving Alaric farther away from Ashlynn, deeper into the depths of the huge catacomb.

Endeavoring to keep the lunatic talking, Alaric asked, "What secret?" As he jumped atop a huge granite monument some ten feet high.

"She was leaving me!" Androu screeched, leaping up beside Alaric as the ancient Vampire dove to the floor.

Jumping to his feet, barely missing a flying slash of his Maker's sword, Alaric grabbed a twisted piece of iron off of the dirt floor, raising it just in time to block another wild swing of Androu's silver sword.

"She was following *you!*" Androu suddenly awakened from his demented stupor and with an impressive display of thrusts, parries, and jabs pushed Alaric backward until the backs of his knees struck stone.

Punctuating every move with more madness, Androu railed on, "I had no choice. She took every option away from me. She was sailing out the very next day. Chasing after you as she always did. Never seeing what was right in front of her. Me! The man who loved her enough to do what was necessary."

Struggling to stay upright, feeling his balance listing to

the rear, Alaric's arms swung wide, flapping in circles, the iron poker he was using as a weapon flying through the air. With one last jab of the tip of his sword into the Alaric's chest, Androu forced him over the granite ledge and into a circular brick-walled hole in the ground.

Falling so quickly all he could do was throw out his arms and hope for the best, Alaric's hand made contact with something short and hard with sharp edges sticking from the wall of the hole. Ignoring the searing pain that cut through his palm and raged through his arm setting fire to his dislocated shoulder, the ancient Vampire bellowed, "I'm not dead yet, you bloody murderer."

Looking up, he nearly lost his grip as Androu sat on the ledge Alaric had just fallen over, gazed into the hole and smiled. "It's better this way," he seemed to be commiserating. "It is truly horrible to see the woman you love beheaded. Trust me when I say it broke my heart…"

"As well as your mind," Alaric growled, shoving the healing magic Carrick had taught him to use into his shoulder as he began to swing his body back and forth.

"You may be right, but I prevailed. I stole Brygid's head from the pike outside the Duke of Argyll's stronghold in the very castle of my Beloved's kin and I carry it with me as a reminder of her."

Scarcely believing what his Maker was saying, Alaric was shocked to his very core when Androu added, "And as such, I shall leave your Bloodmate's, your Ashlynn's, head by her body for you to keep to remember, a daily memento of your failing."

Frenzied rage, unlike anything he'd ever known, exploded within Alaric. Raising his free hand, he shot Dragon fire at his Maker as he swung his body with such force that the sounds of the tendons in his arm and shoulder echoed to the depths of what he had figured out was an old well.

With one last swing, Alaric released his hold on the metal, whizzed like an arrow shot from a bow towards the flickering shadows above and landed with a roll on the dirt-covered floor. Racing towards Ashlynn, the mocking sounds of Androu's voice filling the crypt, Alaric burst through the stone archway, fired a deadly stream of Dragon fire at the raised blade of Androu's sword and launched himself into the air as the grip flew from his Maker's hand.

Throwing his shoulder into Androu's chest, Alaric wrapped his arms around his Maker's chest tackling the deranged one with a loud thud onto the hard, earthen floor. Straddling Androu's chest, Alaric pummeled his face with one punch after another. Over and over he beat upon the other Vampire's flesh until it was little more than a bloody pulp and broken bones.

Slamming his hands over Androu's ears, Alaric roared, "To the depths of Hell I relegate what little remains of your soul. May the Devil show you no mercy."

Ripping the head of his Maker from his body, Alaric threw Androu's head against the unforgiving stone wall, watching dispassionately as blood and gore flew in every direction as a loud crack of what sounded like thunder reverberated through the mausoleum releasing the magic Androu had been using. Jumping to his feet, Alaric raced to Ashlynn.

Waking from whatever spell Androu had suspended her within, her brown eyes slowly regained their usual sparkle as Alaric lifted her into his arms and carried her out into the cool night air. Speeding towards his bike, the ancient Vampire's heart was nearly filled to bursting with love as Ashlynn snuggled close and sighed, "I knew you'd come. I never had any doubt." Then laying her hand over his heart teased, "I'll even deal with the blood and pieces of body parts on your clothes." She kissed his jaw. "But only until we get home and you take a shower. I don't want even a little part of Captain Cuckoo Pants anywhere near us."

16

Living in a hotel was not all it was cracked up to be, not even in the penthouse suite of the Ritz Carlton. Ashlynn was ready to find a home that she and Alaric could make their own. Over the last few weeks since the fire at *CRAVE* and what she was calling 'Androu's Looney Escapade' to keep things light, they had looked at no less than ten estates, places so big they made her head spin and still Alaric thought they needed something bigger.

"It has to be perfect," he continued to say. "I never want you to give up your career. I can feel how very much it means to you. That means whatever house we find must be close to the hospital, but still far enough away that we won't constantly have visitors."

She knew Alaric was talking about Ruari, Sampson and Leslie since they'd been calling and dropping but to check on them nearly every day. It didn't take a Brainiac to see that her Vampire was tired of all the togetherness, especially when every other word out of Leslie's mouth was, "When are y'all gonna make me an auntie?"

Sure, they'd had the discussion that they could have

children, whether she remained human or became Vampire, something that was a real shocker to Ashlynn, but also made her very happy. She'd always wanted a big family, at least two girls and two boys, and the way she and Alaric were, well, 'practicing,' she had no doubt it was going to happen sooner rather than later.

All her questions had been answered. Alaric was nothing if not patient and kind. No matter when or where she thought of something she wanted to ask him, her Vampire stopped everything to make sure she got the information she needed to be comfortable with the new life she was about to step into.

Although she was more than ready to become a Vampire, Alaric had insisted she take time to think about it, to gather all the facts and after they were properly wed, they would revisit her decision. Until that time, she was finding new and erotic ways to take sips of his blood. That way, if he continued to put her off, at least she knew she would still be with the man she loved forever.

Crossing the living room heading towards the study, she added a little extra sway to the swing of her hips as she sidled up to Alaric's desk and with an extremely breathy, very exaggerated Texas drawl enticed, "Isn't it time for a break, Big Guy."

Pulling her into his lap, Alaric had just begun to tease and tempt her with soft, lingering kisses on her neck when his phone rang. She watched as he looked at the screen then scoffed as he turned the screen towards her so she could see that the caller ID read, 'UNKNOWN CALLER'. Smiling a devilish smile and winking, Alaric touched the speaker icon and answered, "Well, hello, Clarence, to what do I owe this honor."

"I hear congratulations are in order," the Legendary

Enforcer replied. "Finding one's Bloodmate is rare indeed. A treasure you should not take for granted."

Pulling her close and kissing the tip of her nose, Ash smiled as she listened to Alaric assure Clarence, "On that, we agree. Although, I think you were debating whether you'd have to have Mateo take my head or not. Didi you really think I had gone rogue?"

"The Thirst can be a deadly thing," Clarence's tone held its usual steel as he continued. "I have read of rampaging Vampires taking out whole towns and villages trying to quench their Thirst, looking for their mystical Bloodmate." The Enforcer cleared his throat. "I'm not sure if you're aware or not, but you are the fifth such case of the mythical Thirst leading to the appearance of a Super's Bloodmate in just the last few months."

"I hadn't heard anything about it, but I will lift my champagne glass to them at our wedding." Alaric chuckled.

"Don't you find it odd, that we have gone millennium after millennium without witnessing such an occurrence and now, like magic, they are here?" Clarence continued to push.

"He's angling at something," Alaric's words flowed through her mind. *"Not that I care, he always was rather full of himself,"* he smiled. *"We are together. My world is perfect. I want for no more."*

His words made Ash's heart beat faster and her body warm with the need to once again have her Vampire all to herself. She knew he had heard her thoughts by the way his eyes turned a seductive hue of gunmetal gray.

Trying not to laugh out loud as Alaric answered the Vampire on the phone, Ash buried her face in Alaric's shoulder as he joked, "That's why they pay you the big bucks, Clarence Collins, Legendary Enforcer of the Directive. I trust you'll get to the bottom of it."

Not waiting for an answer, her soon-to-be husband not only disconnected the call but also turned off his phone, and pushed her farther back onto the desk.

Standing between her thighs, his erection pushing against the denim of his jeans, Alaric kissed the tip of her nose as he whispered, "Vampire kind will be a helluva lot better if many more Bloodmates appear. I only hope they find the same love and happiness that I have found in you, Ashlynn, my sweet."

"And I in you, Alaric, my love." Running her hands over the dragon tattoo that covered the entire left side of his body, her fingers grazed the beast's jaw as she added, "Let me show you how much."

17

———

Continuing his exploration of Ashlynn's neck, paying special attention to every healing mark he'd left on her tender flesh, Alaric loved her moans and mewls. They only served to make him love her more if that was even possible. Moving to her shoulder, he tasted all he could of his Bloodmate, always finding something new and exciting about the only woman in all the world who completed him – body, heart, and soul.

Kissing, tasting, and nibbling, he removed her top and then her bra, reminding himself to continue the discussion about her staying gloriously naked every moment they were together whenever they came up for air, Alaric moved to her waiting breasts, drawing an already swollen, dusty rose nipple into his mouth. Lavishing her heated skin, he pulled as much of her flesh into his mouth as he could, teasing her with his fangs until she arched her back, begging, "Please, Alaric...please, taste me..."

Letting his fangs pierce her flesh, he took the tiniest of sips, letting it dance on his tongue as they both panted from the fire of their union. Pulse racing, drowning in the intoxicating scent of buttercups and poppies warmed by the sun, Alaric knew that no matter how long they lived, he would never tire of the woman coming undone in his arms.

Pushing Ashlynn still farther back onto the desktop, laying her back as he went, Alaric had to take a moment to look at the beautiful woman the gods had seen fit to send to him. Naked from the waist up, lips swollen from his kisses, skin flushed from her excitement, nipples pebbled and pointing to the ceiling, his marks of possession adding to her glow... there was no denying that his Bloodmate was *absolute perfection.*

Reaching for the waistband of her shorts, easily sliding them over her hips and down her legs, Alaric's cock jumped as he realized she had been listening to his suggestions and on this occasion had gone without panties. Completely bare, only for him, his sassy mate, the love of his very long life, lifted her foot, rubbing his rock-hard cock through the worn denim of his jeans. Unable to stop the roll of his hips, Alaric added to the delicious friction Ashlynn applied, having to pull back before he reached the inevitable point of no return. Grinning at the splendid beauty before him, Alaric knew beyond all doubt that the day would never dawn when his Ashlynn didn't set his blood ablaze and make all thought flee from his mind.

Laying his hand on her stomach, Alaric caressed and massaged as he slowly moved towards her pussy. Heat from her arousal stung his fingers the closer he got. Lifting her hips as his fingers slid over the wet proof of her arousal, he chuckled as his feisty mate tried to force his fingers where she needed them the most.

"Patience, my sweet, I need so very much to enjoy you," Alaric cooed, snickering as he was rewarded with one of her playful pouts that nearly had him abandoning his current course in favor of kissing that oh-so-tempting puffy bottom lip of hers, however, the promise of her succulent taste on his tongue won the battle.

Watching as she slowly licked both her index fingers, then her thumbs, before slowly moving her hands to her breasts, Alaric's even breathing became pants of impatience when she took her nipples between her glistening digits and teased them until they hardened even more. With his cock threatening to rip through the fabric, Alaric bent at the waist, pulled to her body like a magnet to metal, and began placing tiny kisses along the outer lips of her already hot and wet pussy. Reaching the top of her slit, he watched as over and over she worked her nipples fighting to keep her eyes open as well as to catch her breath. Blowing a puff of air onto her engorged nub, he was rewarded with the upward jerk of her hips as she moaned while looking right into his eyes.

"Alaric…" His name on her lips pushed him to a place only his Ashlynn could take him, a place where only they existed, where no one could ever interfere.

Touching her clit with the tip of his tongue, while blowing more little puffs of air on the tiny aroused bundle of nerves, Alaric's heart sang as Ashlynn's fingers tangled in his hair, pulling so hard he saw stars. Pushing his tongue between her swollen lips, her taste exploded on his tongue as flashes of light and swirls of color burst before his eyes from a single taste of his mate.

Pushing one finger inside her pussy, then another, pumping in and out, driving her higher and higher as he tasted all she had to give, Alaric separated her outer lips and drove his tongue into Ashlynn's body with one smooth thrust. Her back bowed off the desk, and her legs flew onto his shoulders. She lifted her bottom higher and higher, pushing his tongue farther into her pulsing channel as her head thrashed from side-to-side and she screamed his name.

Loving her responsiveness, constantly amazed by her absolute abandon and trust in him to take care of her, there was no doubt in Alaric's mind that Ashlynn was his perfect match in every way. If they lived forever, he would spend it by her side, loving her more with every beat of his heart.

Continuing to fuck her with his tongue while teasing her clit with his thumb, Alaric enjoyed his Bloodmate too much for it end. Backing off, he flattened his tongue, placed it at the bottom of her slit and at an excruciating slow pace, licked all the way up to her clit. Once again sucking her engorged nub between his fangs, he worried it with the tip of his tongue until Ashlynn ground her hips against his face and dug her heels into his back. Alternating between fucking her with his tongue and licking her like the most decadent sorbet in the world, by the time he was ready for her to come the first time, Ashlynn was speaking in tongues and squeezing his head tightly with her lovely, soft thighs.

Licking her long and slow from bottom to top, sucked her clit into his mouth, but this time bit down with his flat front teeth on her sensitive little nub as he thrust his fingers into her wanting channel, curling the tips to reach her very sensitive bundle of nerves at the top. Pushing Ashlynn, feeling her come with such force, Alaric lapped at the honey flowing from her pussy, having his fill until he slowly suckled her back to earth.

Immeasurable pride filled his entire being, as once again Ashlynn graced him with his name upon her lips in a sweet sign of contentment, "Alaric…"

"Yes, my sweet?"

"I love you." Her voice just a whisper for only his ears as she laid still, completely relaxed, eyes still closed.

"And I love you, my beautiful Ashlynn."

Positioning his cock against her swollen, flushed lips, rubbing the head slowly against her clit as it continued to peek out from its hood, Alaric coated himself with her essence. Slowly pushing into her weeping channel, he stopped when just the head of his cock lay inside.

Contracting, pulling him deeper inside, he followed her lead, slowly pushing inch by inch into her body, teasing them both until they were once again panting, their skin slick with sweat. Touching the top of her womb, Alaric held completely still, savoring the feel of her body contracting around his pulsing cock, riding the razor's edge between control and complete abandon. Her inner walls massaged his erection until his cock throbbed with the need to come.

Every time with Ashlynn was like the first, something to be savored, something to be treasured. He dreamt of staying inside her forever, held together by the perfect union that can only happen when one is truly made for the other. The only problem he could see was if he didn't move he would come before she was ready again, and there would never be a time her pleasure was not the most important thing.

Slowly pulling out, Alaric hovered at her opening. One slight movement and he would have slipped from the heaven that was his Ashlynn. Pushing forward, watching as his hard, cock disappeared into her pussy, the sight causing his balls to draw up tight, he could no longer hold back. Their rhythm increased, each stroke of his cock rubbed against her feminine walls. His vision blurred. His heart beat out of control. Sweat rolled down his back. He would never get enough of her.

Leaning forward, Alaric palmed her breasts, teasing her nipples with his thumbs and forefingers until Ashlynn threw back her head, pushing her breasts farther into his hands. Feeling his release racing to its end, his need for her to come one more time before he filled her with his seed overtook the ancient Vampire. Reaching between them, using his thumb to rub circles over her clit, he drove her higher and higher until she was right on the edge of surrender.

Using his free hand, he slid it under her shoulders and lifted her chest to his. Watching her face, falling more in love with her total surrender she threw back her head and screamed her release, Alaric held on with his legendary steely control as Ashlynn milked his cock with such force he had no doubt the top of his head would surely fly off.

Continuing his sensual assault, harder and faster he thrust into Ashlynn as over and over she climaxed. His cock grew thicker...harder... filling her completely. Holding her tight, kissing the skin over her thundering pulse as he whispered, *"I love you with all that I am,"* into her mind, Alaric pushed his fangs through her porcelain skin at the exact second that he rolled his hips, and bumped the bundle of nerves at the top of her channel.

Exploding together, Ashlynn wailed his name as he drank from her neck and emptied himself into her body. There was absolutely no doubt in the ancient Vampire's mind that the earth moved when he was with his Ashlynn.

Gently laying his mate back onto the desk, Alaric leaned over her sweat-slicked, totally relaxed body and kissed her lips as her breathing returned to normal. "I really hate that you can regulate your breathing so quickly," Ashlynn asked, her breathy tone making his cock start to harden again. "I can't wait until I can do that, too."

"But, I like you out of breath and completely replete from our lovemaking. It's one of the things I live for."

"If I could raise my arm, I'd swat you for that. But, I'm so relaxed that I feel boneless." Her chuckle more throaty than usual because she'd been screaming in pleasure.

"Let's have a bath, my love. What do you say?" he asked as he lifted her into his arms and was rewarded with a purr as she curled into his chest.

"Sounds wonderful," she whispered into his chest.

Walking through the penthouse, Alaric stopped at the wall of glass and turned towards the setting sun. Looking out over the horizon, he saw nothing but the possibility of more happiness than he'd ever known existed.

Kissing the top of Ashlynn's head, he murmured, "I love you, Ashlynn Annalisa Aimsleigh with everything that I am."

Raising her head and cupping his cheek, the love of his life smiled that smile that reached right into his chest and wrapped around his heart as she added, "And I love you, Alaric, to the moon and beyond, forever and always."

Holding her tight, he echoed, "Yes, my love, forever and always."

CHECK OUT ANOTHER KICK ASS VAMP!

VIKTOR:
Heart of Her King
Kings of the Blood, Book 1

The warrior known as Viktoras lay atop the highest mountain, the point of the village closest to the gods, as the sun scorched his bare skin. He waited, spread eagle, wrists and ankles bound to the stakes that had been driven into the dry, brittle earth by his comrades. Those he'd fought beside, bled beside, and swung his sword to defend. This brave soldier had been sentenced to the foulest punishment of their kind. Left to wither away, a slave to the elements, a feast for the vermin.

He thought about the years of his life, the thrill of the victories and the pain of the defeats, all only memories to take to his grave as he felt blisters form upon his searing flesh. He relived every moment of his trial; a farce set upon him by his enemies, led by the weak-minded commander of their sister clan, Bjorn. Such a big name for such a small man. The same coward who'd left his men to die while he ran in fear when faced with their most blood-thirsty adversary.

Bjorn had come to the trial prepared. The traitor had called upon his goddess, Eris – the ruler of chaos, strife and discord, who lent him the power to stand before their Council of Ancestors and provide false testimony against Viktoras. The turncoat assured a conviction against the mighty warrior with a glint in his eye and a snarl upon his lips. Viktoras' men shouted from the gallery, screaming at the injustice before them, telling and retelling the true story of the battle they'd just survived. Their Supreme Commander, however, stood stoic, unwilling to lower himself to be a party to the charade playing out before him.

The only defense Viktoras waged for himself was to the gods. Praying to the goddess of war and wisdom continually from the first day of his incarceration, begging for her guidance. Every unanswered plea was an arrow to his heart. He'd been left to suffer in silence...alone...a doomed man. Sure that his appeals for justice had fallen upon the deaf ears of the goddess Athena, the warrior began praying directly to Zeus. He asked the Father of the Gods to shine light and honesty on the travesty before him, while hour after hour he listened to tainted testimony planted by his enemies.

Finally, the time came for his generals to take the stand. Roman, his second-in-command and friend since childhood, spoke of Viktoras' bravery and valor. The general explained how Viktoras had led the charge against their enemies, never asking even the lowliest of their ranks to do anything he himself, had not already accomplished. Achilles, a brigadier general and named for his father, spoke of the many wounded their supreme commander and friend carried to the medics while continuing to fight the thundering hordes descending upon them from all sides. The last allowed to speak was Bain, the eldest of the Michaelidis family and a newly promoted general. He focused on the man beyond the battlefield, explaining in excruciating detail the special care

Viktoras took of the women and children left without a man of the family due to their country's constant conflicts.

The commander watched the faces of each member of the council as his friends and comrades gave testimony. The corrupt lawgivers showed no emotion, gave no indication they were even listening, only looked over the crowd as if taking attendance. When they left to deliberate, Viktoras knew the outcome was a forgone conclusion. His fate had been decided the moment the cold steel shackles were clamped tightly upon his wrists and ankles. The trial was only a formality, a way for his enemies to justify his murder. They wanted to avoid an uprising from those who would remain loyal to the great Supreme Commander, Viktoras.

No matter his belief in the doom he faced, Viktoras still prayed to the almighty Zeus, knowing if a miracle was to be bestowed upon him, it would be by the King of the Gods. Long after the fateful verdict had been delivered, while the mighty warrior sat waiting for the executioner, a light shown from above and a voice unlike any Viktoras had ever heard reverberated off the stone walls of his cell.

"You have remained loyal, my child, even unto the end. A fate worse than most has befallen you and it is true that life as you know it will soon be forfeit, but this is not the end, great warrior. You are destined for far greater things.

"Your heart will cease to beat. Your lungs will cease to draw breath. You will be buried in a traitor's grave—but do not fret. Thirty days will come and go while your body rests and transforms. As the sun touches the horizon on the night of the thirty-first day, you shall rise. Your heart will again beat. Your lungs will again draw breath and you, my loyal servant, will be made immortal. You will be known as 'The Unum', The One, the first King of the Blood. You will serve a higher purpose. You will smite the enemies that mortals cannot. You will live in resurrection as

you lived in life, an unknown hero amongst the masses with a worth beyond all imagination.

"Those loyal to you in life may also be called into service. It is a choice you will have to make, for only you will have the power to make them immortal, to make them future Kings of the Blood. Together, you and yours will form a fraternity unlike any other, with the sole purpose of protecting those who cannot protect themselves.

"As with everything, there is a price and yours is twofold. Although you will live and thrive as you always have, you will also need to consume life's essence once every new moon. The darkest night of the month at the darkest time of the night is when you shall feed. It should be given willingly and accepted gratefully. Take only the small amount you need to replenish the powers bestowed upon you and leave your donor unblemished.

"Lastly, you will have a mate, your custos animae, *the keeper of your heart. The one woman in all the world who can save your doomed soul and breathe life into your dead heart. She will be the perfect complement to your darkness, a light that shines so brightly there are no shadows for you to hide behind. She will know your every weakness, share your every secret, and accept you for all that you are. This gift of the gods will be your only nourishment from the moment of her recognition of you. You will know when this woman is born. You will feel it in the depths of your soul, but you must wait for her. When the time is right, she will come to you. The mating must be completed before nightfall of your three thousandth year or you will cease to exist. You will return to the ether from whence you came, ashes to ashes and dust to dust. You will enter the Elysian Fields and live a hero's afterlife.*

"Our time is up, my supreme commander. The guards approach. Your day of death is nigh. Know that I am watching and waiting. Know that your purpose is true and just, blessed by

not only the King of the Gods but by the entire Pantheon. Go forth, brave warrior, die so that you might live and fulfill your honor bound destiny."

In the blink of an eye, the light from above and the voice of Zeus disappeared as if they had never existed. The guards arrived as predicted and once again locked steel shackles on his wrists and ankles, but this time, he was taken to the top of the mountain and left to die.

Days passed. His strength waned. He knew the end was near but held out hope that what Zeus had promised would come to pass. Viktoras knew he was to serve a greater purpose. He would be true to his mission and do as the King of the Gods had commanded, while also hunting down those responsible for his premature death. Bjorn and the lawgivers would feel the cold, harsh steel of his blade upon their necks. He would watch the life fade from their eyes. Their blood would pay the debt.

With that one last thought, the supreme commander gave his spirit over to the gods and the true story of Viktor Katsaros began....

READ THE WHOLE STORY RIGHT HERE!

"Dammit, Grace, pick up the phone," she growled through gritted teeth at the third voicemail she'd had to listen to in the last five minutes.

"Everything okay, Kyndel?' Barney, the *nice* guy in her office, asked.

"Yeah, everything's fine. Just trying to find Grace."

"Oh! Anything I can help with?"

Kyndel thought about telling him her troubles, but Barney had been spending an inordinate amount of time in her office lately. At first, she'd thought he was just being nice, but then he joined her hiking group, and just yesterday he showed up with her favorite no whip, nonfat, iced white chocolate mocha from the *frou frou* coffee shop on the corner. It had been then Kyndel realized she was Barney's newest crush. It had been a long time between boyfriends and Barney was nice, but...um...*no*. As flattered as she was, there was no way she was having an office romance.

'Don't shit where you eat' was one of the pieces of sage advice Granny had given her just after graduation. Not that it ever truly made sense to Kyndel, but she got the gist of it... keep your personal life *out* of the office.

She saw the puppy dog look on Barney's face and hated to crush his spirit, but Kyndel decided a brisk walk home would be better than leading the poor fellow on, in *any* way.

"No but thank you so much." Then, to make sure he got the hint and skedaddled, she added, "Have a nice a week-end," before turning her chair and dialing Grace's office for the third time.

Voicemail *again*. Time to pack up and get the heck outta dodge before someone found something else for her to do. Bag on shoulder, scowl on face, and more than a little disgusted, Kyndel headed out of the office.

*Never loan Grace the car... Never loan Grace the car...*was the mantra playing on a loop in Kyndel's mind. She was madder than a wet hen and getting hotter by the minute. It was *no fun* to walk home after ten hours of work. *No fun* to be abandoned and forgotten by the best friend she'd loaned her car to. *No fun* to make the five-block journey past the park...in the dark.

At twenty-six, she rarely admitted her fear of the dark and held her aunts responsible for the phobia. Had they not made her watch 'The Brain Eaters' when she was only six years old, Kyndel was positive everything would've been just fine. It wasn't that she believed aliens would set loose a horde of parasites to eat every human brain on the planet; she had a *little* more sense than that. It was the feeling of being watched...like someone was hiding in the shadows, just waiting for an opportunity to scare the living daylights out of her. At the mere thought of her 'phantom stalker', the hair stood up at the nape of her neck and she walked a bit faster.

A sudden *thud,* and what sounded like footsteps pounding on the hard ground, had her stopping in her tracks. "What the...?" She gasped, opening her eyes wide, hoping it would help her see through the shadows.

Several tense seconds later—that felt like damn near forever—and Kyndel moved again. This time, her eyes slid side-to-side like the stupid black and white cat clock her granny used to have in the kitchen.

The farther she got from where she'd heard the 'thump', the easier it was to convince herself it had just been kids sneaking into the park after hours. Manlove Park was a well-known make out spot for teenagers. There might've even been a time after moving to the city when Kyndel herself had been convinced to take a walk on the wild side, but that was a story for another day.

Shoot, now I wouldn't know the wild side if I tripped and fell in it.

It had been almost a year since she'd dated the muscle-headed jock from the gym. Three long, tortuous dates and all because he had an incredible body. Of course, dating the douche bag had come at a price. She'd spent the entire time listening to him drone on about his body parts...*and not the good ones*...and *only* when he wasn't checking out every other woman in the joint.

It wasn't that he'd hurt her feelings. Kyndel knew who she was and had never been under the misconception she would be Miss America. She had a few extra pounds and her curves had curves, but she was cute and had a brain, something not everyone could claim. What had pissed her off the most about dating Vinnie was, she'd wasted three whole evenings of her life that she could never get back. The one compliment the jerk had given her had been about her skin; he thought it was beautiful. Her granny always called her complexion peaches and cream and said her freckles added character.

Yeah, 'cause I need more of that.

She sighed as she thought about how much of her youth she'd wasted hating those tiny brown spots, until the day she realized they weren't going anywhere. It was time to buck up and learn to love them, or stop looking in the mirror. From that day forward, she stopped using makeup to cover them and embraced her 'freckled-self'. She also learned to accept her curves. *If ya don't like em, don't look at em* was her motto. For the most part, she ate right and worked out at least three times a week. But dammit if she didn't love her Ben and Jerry's Cherry Garcia and someone would lose a hand if they tried to take it from her.

A loud *'thud'* echoed between the buildings. Kyndel stumbled to a stop. She looked and listened. The longer she thought about what she'd heard, the easier it was for her to convince herself someone had yelled for help. So, for the second time in about as many minutes, she searched the inky shadows for signs of life. Her anxiety level quadrupled the longer she stood still. She wanted to scream when only the sound of leaves rustling across the sidewalk and the occasional car passing by reached her ears.

Disgusted, she grumbled aloud, "You've gone bonkers, Kyn." The sound of her own voice somehow calmed her rankled nerves and she added, "Get to stepping, girlie."

The clicking of her heels bounced off the brick wall of the library as she hurried past. Resuming her original mantra, she added *Must kill Grace* at the end for good measure.

"I swear when I get my hands on..."

Her words were cut short as the unmistakable sound of a man groaning came from the shadows.

A chill skittered down her spine.

Goose bumps covered her arms.

She counted to three, unable to move...simply listening...praying it was only her imagination. One deep breath later, she slid her right foot forward, prepared to make a beeline for home at a high rate of speed.

The groan came again. Closer than before. More desperate...almost pleading.

The need to help the injured grew within her. Turning towards the darkness, Kyndel searched for the source of the noise.

Shaking so much her teeth chattered, she looked for any sign of the man she *knew* needed her help.

"It's time to make a decision, Kyndel. Fight or flight. What's it gonna be? God knows standing like a bump on a log isn't solving a *damn* thing."

Flight won. She turned, almost running, her satchel clutched tightly to her side like a lifeline.

"Keep your head up and eyes front. Home's only a few blocks away," she reassured herself, with the promise of snatching her best friend bald for the stupid mess she was in.

Feeling guilty and worried for Grace, her heart at war with her brain, Kyndel thought aloud, "Hope everything's okay..."

Grace had always been a little scatter-brained, but she'd never just *forgotten* Kyndel before. It bothered her that there'd been no answer at Grace's office or on her cellphone when Kyndel had tried to track her down before leaving the office. She'd even taken a chance and tried her own home because Grace had a key, but only got voicemail there, too. It was a war between anger and worry that accompanied most of her thoughts about her friend lately.

The running joke was that Grace spent most of her time hooking up with eligible bachelors she met at work. The good Lord *knew* her bestie was gorgeous; five foot nine, long raven hair, blue eyes, and a curvy body without an extra ounce of fat. To top it off, she was a first-year lawyer, with a promising career. Grace had it all...brains and beauty, the total package.

Giggling nervously, she gave herself a mental swat to the back of the head. She didn't want anything bad to happen to Grace, just a bump or bruise, even a hangnail would explain being left. If she really had just forgotten, Kyndel was going to be *pissed* and more than a little hurt.

The shadows seemed to be closing in. Fear pushed Kyndel until she was almost jogging in her sensible work heels. Looking over her shoulder, the toe of her shoe caught an uneven piece of concrete, and from one heartbeat to the next, she was falling forward. Arms flailing, mouth stretched wide in a wordless scream, the sidewalk racing toward her face, everything around her seemed to happen in slow motion. All she could think was *that's gonna leave a mark.*

Bracing for impact, she squeezed her eyes tight and prayed...then nothing happened. Opening one eye, then the other, Kyndel found herself hanging above the sidewalk, looking at a pair of the biggest feet she had ever seen—and they were sexy.

Sexy feet? I really am losing it. Wait! Why the hell am I above the concrete?

Warmth radiated from the perfectly muscled arm

wrapped around her midsection. Goose bumps emanated from the extra-large hand holding firmly to her blouse, just a little too close to her breast.

She wiggled to change position, the cushion of her well-rounded ass finding the ridges of an incredibly hard set of abs. She trembled. Her heart raced. Just the thought of the man that could hold her upright made up for all her previous mishaps.

Within just a few seconds, Kyndel's world turned on its axis. The scenery blurred as she was effortlessly spun around and immediately found herself sitting atop the body of her rescuer, looking at faded denim covering extremely muscular thighs. Laughing aloud, she asked herself, *"Wonder what part I'll see next?*

The same muscled arm that had saved her face from certain demise now kept her upright. She did a one-eighty, draped her legs over his thighs, with her knees barely touching the sidewalk, and got her first look at the top half of her rescuer. All she could do was gape. He was absolutely the most handsome man she'd ever seen, with features that looked like they'd been carved by expert hands.

Even with his eyes closed, he gave off the distinctive air of authority. The dim light highlighted his high cheekbones and aristocratic nose, adding to the power she felt radiating from his every pore. His perfectly formed lips made visions of passionate kisses and hot sweaty nights dance through her brain. It didn't help that all he had on was a pair of well-worn blue jeans.

She imagined that denim riding low on his tapered hips when he stood, highlighting the incredibly sexy dimples that sat on the front of his hips. She absolutely knew without looking they were there, and that simple bit of knowledge made her temperature rise another degree, despite the cool breeze.

At the touch of her fingertips against the cool skin of his neck, an electric current arced between them. Flashes of light burst before her eyes. She blinked to clear her vision, then felt for his pulse, strong and steady against her digit. Heat rose from his skin, making her worry he might have a fever. Her eyes wandered down his well-toned body. She scoffed, unsuccessfully trying to convince herself she was only checking for further injury.

Who the hell do you think you're fooling?

She continued her perusal, taking note of his massive shoulders and a chest that could've been sculpted from granite. The light smattering of hair that glistened in the shards of light from the streetlamps emphasized his nipples, which were pebbled from the cool breeze. Her mouth watered and her pulse raced.

What the hell is it about this guy? Is he doused in pheromones? Or am I in heat?

Her eyes landed on the best set of abs she'd ever seen. Unable, or maybe it was unwilling, to stop her hand, she traced the defined lines of his eight-pack, mesmerized by the feel of his skin beneath her fingers. The electricity continued to flow between them. The sound of a horn in the distance pulled her from her musing and brought her current situation into the glaring light of reality. The sexy man that had kept her from breaking her face on the concrete was out cold, and she was paying him back by sitting on his lap and copping a feel.

She scrambled to her feet, surprised her rescuer hadn't moved an inch during her less than graceful attempt to remove her butt from his lap. But there he lay, unmoving, except for the rise and fall of his chest. The longer he remained unconscious, the more panicked she became.

Looking up and down the street and cursing Grace for the hundredth time, Kyndel wished for her car. First Aid class had taught her *never* to move an injured person unless you knew what was wrong. Not that she could pick him up and carry him, anyway. The dude was *HUGE*. At least six foot-three or four, and his muscles had muscles. She prayed he hadn't hit his head on the sidewalk. A concussion could be really bad if not treated.

"You're worried about a concussion now?" She scolded herself. "You've been drooling over the guy while his head is lying on the cold, hard sidewalk. Brilliant, Kyn, just brilliant." Reaching for her satchel, she grabbed her old sorority sweatshirt from inside, wadded it up, and knelt forward to lift his head.

Her fingers tangled in his soft, brown hair. The scattered shards of light made it look like melted chocolate flowing over her skin.

Would it shine in the sun or maybe have highlights? Some lighter brown mixed with red, even a few blond streaks woven throughout?

The silky softness of his tresses turned to something wet and sticky.

Blood!

Kyndel gulped. Panic seized the breath in her lungs as the true severity of the situation smacked her in the face. She fought to keep her calm. Now, there was absolutely no denying he needed medical attention. Reaching into her bag and cursing herself for not thinking of it sooner, she dug around for her cellphone.

Coming up empty-handed, she instantly remembered plugging it into her car charger the night before, not giving it the slightest thought until that moment. Cursing and threatening death to anyone in the immediate vicinity, she sat back on her heels and thought.

All I know to do is run down the street for help.

Looking at the fallen man, then in the direction of the Mini Mart, she reasoned he'd probably be okay. She'd be gone five minutes...*tops*. Run in, use the phone, run back. It all seemed very logical, but fear something would happen to him in her absence kept her in place.

This guy was important to her. That alone had all her red flags flying and bells and whistles screaming in her brain. She tried to push her feelings aside and look at the situation with logic, but that was like holding back a freight train with her pinky finger...*not gonna happen*. Besides, her granny would most definitely haunt her and probably kick her butt if she turned her back on someone who needed help.

"No one's gonna mess with this behemoth, even if he *is* unconscious," she reassured herself. "He probably doesn't have a wallet to steal anyway."

Should she dig in his pockets to try to find one? Some kind of ID?

Nah.

She wasn't keen on trying to explain her hand in his pants if he woke up. Her cheeks warmed at the thought of touching him again.

"What are you doing out at night in just a pair of jeans and bare feet, anyway?" she asked the unconscious man. "Guess it doesn't matter. You need help, whether you're dressed properly or not."

Hooking her satchel over her shoulder, Kyndel stood and took one last look at her 'patient'. Before she had barely moved an inch, a huge, warm hand latched onto her bare ankle.

"What the hell?" she screamed, trying to pull her leg free while looking down to see what new fresh hell had befallen her.

GET THE WHOLE STORY HERE! FOR FREE!

ABOUT JULIA

Find all my stories at JuliaMillsAuthor.com!

Hey Y'all! I'm Julia Mills the New York Times and USA Today Bestselling Author of the Dragon Guard Series. I without a doubt admit to being a sarcastic, southern woman who would rather spend all day laughing than a minute crying. Living with my two most amazing daughters and a menagerie of animals, keeps me busy but I love telling a good story. Now, that I've decided to write the stories running through my brain, life is just a blast!

My beliefs are simple. A good book along with shoes, makeup, and purses will never let a girl down and no hero ever written will compare to my real-life hero, my dad! I'm a sucker for a happy ending, and alpha men make me swoon.

I'm still working on my story, but I promise it will contain as much love and laughter as I can pack into it! Now, go out there and create your own story!!! Dare to Dream! Have the Strength to Try EVERYTHING! Never Look Back!

Take care and Read lots!

I ABSOLUTELY adore stalkers so look me up on Facebook,
sign up for my newsletter at JuliaMillsAuthor.com, and
follow me on BookBub!
Send me a message!
XOXO Julia

ALSO BY JULIA MILLS

Find Them All at JuliaMillsAuthor.com!

*Although this epic journey travels through many Clans, many lands,
and many couples, one thing remains constant -*

Fate Will Not Be Denied.

*Each book is written as a standalone story, but just like M&M's, Lay's
Potato Chips, and my momma's queso, they're better when binged.*

Reading Order for

THE DRAGON GUARD

Her Dragon to Slay

Her Dragon's Fire

Haunted by Her Dragon

For the Love of Her Dragon

Saved by Her Dragon, Dragon Guard

Only for Her Dragon, Dragon Guard

Fighting for Her Dragon, Dragon Guard

Her Dragon's Heart, Dragon Guard

Her Dragon's Soul, Dragon Guard

The Fate of Her Dragon

Her Dragon's No Angel

Her Dragon, His Demon

Resurrecting Her Dragon

The Scars of Her Dragon

Her Mad Dragon

Tears for Her Dragon

Guarding Her Dragon

Sassing Her Dragon

Kiss of Her Dragon

Claws, Class, and a Whole Lotta Sass

Dragon with the Girl Tattoo

Dragon Down

Twinkle, Twinkle, Sassy Little Star

Dragon Got Your Tongue

Her Dragon's Fury

Dragon in the Mist

Dragon Got Run Over by A Reindeer

Tangled in Tinsel

Cupcake Kisses & Dragon Dreams

Her Dragon's Treasure

Aww Snap, Dragon

Imagine Dragon

Save a Horse, Ride a Dragon

Burn Dragon Burn

She Thinks My Dragon's Sexy

Dreamin' of a White Dragon

Dragon Her Home

Stone Cold Protector

Dragon's Lore

King Outta Water

Dragon, It's Cold Outside

Dragon, Be Mine

Rockin' Around the Dragon, Tree

Savage Protector

Dragon, Take the Wheel

Chestnuts Roasting Over Dragon Fire

Dragon Falling – Dragon Intelligence Agency – Crimson Moon

Dragon Dreaming - – Dragon Intelligence Agency – Crimson Moon

Dragon Out the Tinsel

Unwrapping Her Dragon

Dragons of Destiny

Dragon Him Out to Sea

Dragon Guard Berserkers

BANNING

ASHER

RAYNOR

Ladies of the Sky

Sadie's Shadow

Southern Fried Sass Series

Later Gator

Nosey Rosie

Lazy Daisy

Jamie's Got a Wand

Maidens of Mayhem

That Hound Don't Hunt

That Pig Gonna Fly

That Mule's Got A Kick

That Rex Gotta Roar

That Llama Gonna Spit

That Shark is Red Hot

Up Shift Creek Series

Tree Frog and Her Honey Badger

Doc and Her Dragon

Dusty and Her Dino

The 'Not-Quite' Love Story Series

Vidalia: A 'Not-Quite Vampire Love Story

Phoebe" A 'Not-Quite' Phoenix Love Story

Zoey: A 'Not-Quite' Zombie Love Story

Jax: A 'Not-Quite' Puma Love Story

Heidi: A 'Not-Quite' Hellhound Love Story

Lola: A 'Not-Quite' Witchy Love Story

Sammie Jo: A 'Not-Quite' Shifting Witchy Love Story

Harmony: A 'Not-Quite' Haunted Love Story

Daphne: A 'Not-Quite' VooDoo Gumshoe Love Story

Kings of the Blood

VIKTOR: Heart of Her King ~ Kings of the Blood ~ Book 1

ROMAN: Fury of Her King ~ Kings of the Blood ~ Book2

ACHILLES: Soul of Her King ~ Kings of the Blood ~ Book 3

CAUGHT: A Vampire Blood Courtesan Romance

CONDEMNED: A Vampire Blood Courtesan Romance

MARROK: A Wolf's Hunger

Out of the Ashes: Daughters of Poseidon ~ Book 1

Scorched Ember: Daughters of Poseidon ~ Book 2

Alaric: A Vampire's Thirst

JOIN THE CLAN!

Wanna keep up with all my crazy? Have fun? Win some cool prizes? Get *exclusive* excerpts to upcoming books?
Sign up for my newsletter <u>RIGHT HERE</u>!
Be the FIRST to see new covers, sneak peeks, and best of all, ADVANCED COPIES OF ALL MY BOOKS!!!
Join the group! <u>Julia's Mills' Fan Club on Facebook</u>!
I absolutely LOVE stalkers! Here's all the links! Follow me everywhere!
<u>Newsletter</u>
<u>Website</u>
<u>Facebook</u>
<u>Instagram</u>
<u>Twitter</u>
<u>Pinterest</u>
<u>BookBub</u>
<u>Goodreads</u>

One Night Will Never Be Enough

NO ONE ESCAPES DESTINY.